GW00391471

SHADOW OF

TEMPTATION

Jessie Donovan

This book is a work of fiction. Names, characters, places, and incidents are either the product of the writer's imagination or are used fictitiously, and any resemblance to actual persons, living or dead, business establishments, events, or locales is entirely coincidental.

Shadow of Temptation
Copyright © 2014 Laura Hoak-Kagey
First Edition

Cover Art by Clarissa Yeo of Yocla Designs.

ISBN 13: 978-1942211051

To Joanna
In addition to being my awesome niece, she also came up with the title for this book. Thanks Jojo!

Other Books by Jessie Donovan

The *Feiru*

The Feiru *are a race similar in appearance to humans, but with slight genetic differences…First-born children of* Feiru *mothers have the ability to manipulate elemental energy particles, which, until recently, had been undetectable to human scientists. What type of element they can control—fire, earth, water, or wind—and whether their ability is aggressive or healing in nature is determined by genetics. These* Feiru-*specific abilities are commonly referred to as "elemental magic" amongst their kind.*

…As long as the Feiru *continue to uphold the rules and regulations set forth in The Agreement, and hide their unique abilities and existence from humans, they will be allowed to govern over their own kind. If they violate The Agreement, the* Feiru *liaison offices of the various world governments will meet and devise a plan on how to handle the* Feiru *failures…The primary function of the* Feiru *liaison office is to prevent worldwide paranoia, no matter the cost.*

—Excerpt from the *Feiru* Liaison Training Guide, US Edition

Chapter One

Deemed disbanded in 2004, the Federation League has re-formed and is crawling its way back from obscurity. However, their aim remains the same: to kill or harm anyone who has worked with or for the Asylums for Magical Threats' prison system. Assassinations and arson fires are their main tactics, but any unusual activity that targets a Feiru *(FEY-roo) should be investigated.*

— Case File on the Federation League, Mexico City *Feiru* Liaison Office

Merida, Mexico

Sabrina Ono was about to crack. If she didn't find somewhere private, and soon, she would blow the cover ID she'd worked so hard to craft over the last two years.

And if she let that happen, all of the deaths, all of the destruction, and all of the grief she had caused to innocent humans and *Feiru* alike while undercover would have been for nothing. Sabrina wasn't sure she could handle that amount of guilt if she failed.

Come on, Ono. You can do this. She was this close to finishing her current assignment. No matter what it took, she needed to maintain her life of lies for a few more days.

Harry Watkins, her current team leader, came over to where she was standing and scrutinized her face. "You look like you want to say something, Ono."

She was careful to keep her emotions from her face and voice. "No, sir."

"Right. Then do the scouting I asked for. I want the layout, details, and your suggestions for the best ways to break in to the building by this evening. Once I receive your report, I'll send a follow-up task."

Sabrina nodded. "Is there anything else, sir?"

He studied her a second before waving his hand. "No, you're dismissed."

Careful to keep her face expressionless, Sabrina saluted Watkins, turned, and headed down the street toward the target she needed to scout.

Before she could do her job, she needed to find somewhere to get her shit together. If Watkins had anyone watching her, which was possible with this high-profile assignment, she couldn't show her fragile state or she would be replaced. Sabrina couldn't allow that to happen.

When she was about ten blocks away from where Watkins had dismissed her, she did everything she could to make sure no one was following her, and then she ducked into an abandoned alley. After turning down another side street, she squatted down behind a parked car, put her head in her hands, and focused on breathing in and out to calm her nerves.

She had harmed humans and *Feiru* alike as part of her cover ID over the last two years. Be it scouting a location, gathering intelligence, or helping to divert the attention of human authorities. She may not have pulled a trigger or detonated a bomb, but she was just as responsible as every other cog in the network. She had justified her actions because her end goal was to dismantle the Federation League. In the last few months, she'd finally pinpointed how to do it.

If she could take down Harry Watkins, she believed the organization would start to crumble, creating a weakness her superiors from the *Feiru* Liaison office in Mexico City could use and pounce upon.

Watkins had been training Fed League members on how to select AMT-related targets, how to scout out locations, and finally, how to set successful arson fires without getting caught. But he was much more than just a mercenary paid to train a group of haphazard recruits. She was fairly confident he had a much bigger client bankrolling him, a client she wanted to identify.

Over the last few months, she'd studied the man's habits and even learned the names of some of his closest contacts. With a final push, Sabrina should be able to find out the information she needed to end this assignment. Yet because of Watkins's latest target, she was going to have to up her game and make her final play sooner than she had anticipated.

The reason? In less than a week, Watkins planned to set off a bomb at an elementary school during the day, while the children were still in class.

Sabrina felt tears prick her eyes and she took a deep breath. As the death tally rose, it became harder and harder to rationalize her actions. The death of an elderly *Feiru* woman and several young restaurant workers had shaken her up in recent weeks, and she knew the death of so many children would be her tipping point.

She rubbed her eyes and lifted her head from her hands. There was only one way for her to save the school and get the information she needed about Watkins. She would just have to take a few more risks and make her final move.

If done right, she should be able to stay in her undercover role for at least this week. However, once she foiled the plan to bomb the school, Watkins would quickly be on her ass and she would have to flee.

It wasn't a matter of "if" she could do it—she had to find a way to make it work.

With a last deep breath, Sabrina stood up. She would force herself to go through the motions for a little longer. She would scout the school and file her report, but then she needed to reach out and set up a secret meeting with her superior from the *Feiru* Liaison office. She only had five days to put her operation in place and execute it. She couldn't afford to wait another day.

Sabrina moved to the corner where the alley opened out onto the street and checked to make sure no one had followed her. The coast clear, she went back out on the main street and headed toward the nearby elementary school.

~~*

Once upon a time, Jorge Salazar had had friends, responsibilities, and even a woman he had wanted more than his own life. But then his latent ability had appeared nine months ago, and he'd learned that he was a Shadow-Shifter.

After that, his life had gone to hell.

Betrayal by the woman he loved? Check. Being kidnapped and tortured into working for a sociopath who called herself the Collector? Check.

Hell, about the only thing that hadn't happened to him was castration.

SHADOW OF TEMPTATION

But thanks to some help from DEFEND—an activist group fighting to bring down the Asylums for Magical Threats' prison system for elemental magic users—he'd found a way to escape the Collector, at least for a little while.

The Collector woman had kidnapped his sister and had used her as leverage, making him do things that would haunt him until he died. But a few days ago, DEFEND had rescued his sister, also allowing him to escape. However, his sister's safety had come at a price—he had to agree to track down one of his old colleagues, a man named Harry Watkins, and stop the bastard from setting off any more arson fires.

While the Collector's people would only have noticed his absence a few hours ago, he didn't have much time to carry out his task. The Collector didn't like losing any of her assets, and anyone who tried to escape was hunted down and killed. To date, only two people had ever managed to escape her clutches and avoid death.

Jorge's odds didn't look good.

But he was determined to take care of Watkins before the Collector's soldiers found him. To do that, he needed information from the man in front of him, but his former colleague and friend was being less than helpful.

Jorge pressed his arm more firmly against the man's neck. "You owe me your life, Dylan. Tell me about the next fire, and I'll leave you alone. If you don't, then you'll find out firsthand why I was kicked out of the Fed League."

Dylan merely glared at him.

Jorge gave the man a shake before pinning him back up against the wall. "Don't push your luck. We might've been friends once, but I have a debt to pay, and you know how much importance I put on paying my debts in full. I need to know about Watkins's plans."

Dylan looked him dead in the eye and said nothing. After a long moment, he finally opened his mouth and said, "If you know Watkins, then you know what he'll do to me if I tell you anything."

"Then I'd suggest you tell me and disappear. Changes are coming that you aren't going to like, and listening to my advice will save your ass for the second time in as many years."

Dylan scrutinized his face, and Jorge had to give him credit. The man was cool under pressure.

But Jorge had worked with the man for nearly a year before he'd left the Fed League, and he knew that Dylan only stayed because he had nowhere else to go.

Maybe a suggestion would prod him to reveal Watkins's next target. "Listen, soon Watkins won't be anyone's problem. Until I take care of him, go back to the US. Find a job, go to college, or, hell, live on a friend's couch for all I care. The Fed League is starting to crumble. Do you really want to be around when it does? The *Feiru* High Council isn't going to treat any of you lightly."

His old friend looked unimpressed. "Tell me why you were kicked out, and then I'll believe your message is serious."

"You wouldn't believe me if I told you."

Dylan managed to shrug a shoulder despite Jorge's grip. "Well, then, we're at an impasse because I'm not telling you anything. Despite everything we've gone through, you just vanished without a fucking word."

Jorge hadn't had a choice, but he didn't have time to explain the Collector and her methods. "Whether you believe me or not, contacting you would've endangered your life. And the longer you linger here with me now, the greater the chance you'll find out why I kept my distance."

"Do you know what they say happened to you?"

"I really couldn't give a flying fuck."

Dylan ignored him. "They say you switched sides, and were spying for the AMT Oversight Committee."

"And what makes you think that I didn't?"

"You hated the AMT for torturing your cousin and driving him insane. There's no way you would've helped those bastards."

This was taking too long. He wasn't about to stab his former friend, so Jorge decided to take a chance. "I would kill myself before I helped the AMT, you're right. But I didn't leave by choice. I was forced out. You know the rule about no Fed League member being allowed to have magic?" Dylan nodded. "Well, I sort of inherited some strange abilities, and they wanted me gone."

"Yeah, and I learned how to breath under water. Come on, Jorge, tell me the truth."

What did he have to lose? The Collector would find him sooner or later and kill him. He may as well reveal his powers to one of the few people he'd called a friend. "Fine, asshole. Have you ever heard of a Shadow-Shifter?"

Dylan shook his head. "No."

Considering the stories about his kind had been outlawed by the *Feiru* High Council decades ago, Dylan's answer didn't surprise him.

Jorge could only shift once every twenty-four hours, but he knew from overhearing conversations between Fed League members yesterday that Watkins wasn't due to strike for nearly a week. He could sacrifice one day of not being able to use his abilities if it meant he could find out enough information to help him come up with a plan.

He raised his free arm and said, "Well, they can do this."

He concentrated, relaxing the muscles in his free arm, and started to imagine each cell breaking down. The more he visualized the breakdown of his arm, the more transparent it became until there was a jolt of pain that flashed through his entire body, leaving his arm nothing but a dark, shadowy mist.

At first, Dylan said nothing. But when Jorge drew the shadowy mist tightly together in the shape of his arm and willed it solid, his friend finally said, "Holy shit, Jorge. We all know about elemental magic, but since when do superhero-type powers exist?"

He resisted a sigh and ignored his question. "Now that I've proven the reason I was kicked out, you're going to tell me everything you know about Watkins's upcoming target, and then get the fuck out of Mexico."

Dylan kept staring at his arm. At this rate, he wouldn't get any information. "Dylan, look at me." At first, his former friend didn't do anything. But after giving his old friend a shake, Dylan met his eyes and Jorge continued. "Tell me about the target."

"Well, the rumor is that Watkins is targeting an elementary school."

"I need more than a rumor."

"I do the science stuff, and help with making the bombs. Watkins doesn't tell me anything except how powerful he wants the explosive. I have to rely on rumors for what else is going on."

In the past, everyone who had worked on an assignment had known all the details. Things must have changed in the last nine months. "How confident are you of this rumor?"

Dylan shrugged a shoulder. "Pretty confident. The two people who let it slip have worked in the planning stages in the past with Watkins. I see no reason for them to lie to me."

Despite Dylan's stupidity in staying with the Fed League, he was a lousy liar. That was the reason he'd been assigned the task of bomb maker. Jorge decided he was telling the truth. "So, when is this all supposed to happen?"

"The current target date is five days from now. The bomb should go off in the mid-morning."

"And you didn't think twice about this?"

Dylan's face became serious. "You used to work with the Fed League too, Jorge. You know that if you don't do what they ask, they find a way to make you do it. Making a bomb for some faceless kids is better than seeing my friends tortured in front of me."

Usually the Fed League tortured family, but Dylan didn't have any; his friends meant everything to him.

Jorge had forgotten about that, and he had a split second feeling of guilt for abandoning one of his closest friends. But then he remembered the debt he still owed Aislinn and Neena—the two co-leaders of DEFEND—and he focused. "Which is why heeding my warning and getting the hell away from here is all the better. Maybe you can convince some of your friends to go back to the States with you."

"And what about you, Jorge? What're you going to do?"

"I'm going to stop Watkins, no matter the cost."

Dylan eyed him. "Well, if you make it out alive, you can find me in Houston under the alias Dylan Riker. If you buy me a few beers, maybe I'll forgive you for leaving me."

After his time with the Collector, Jorge had forgotten about friendship. He wanted to say he'd look his old friend up, but he wasn't about to give him false hope. "If I somehow make it out of this alive, I'll consider it. But I won't make any promises."

Dylan studied his face. "You may have ditched me without a word, but if you're in serious trouble, then just ask for my help, and you've got it."

Jorge released his friend and shook his head. "No. The best way you can help me is to give me the address of the next target and then get your ass out of here."

As Dylan stared at him, Jorge started to feel uncomfortable. But just as he was about to repeat his request, Dylan spoke up. "All right. But if I hear that you finish this alive and don't come see me, I'll kick your ass."

The corner of Jorge's mouth ticked up. "I would say that you don't stand a chance, but somehow I don't think that would make a difference."

Dylan grinned. "Good thing you realize that. Now, do you have something to write with or a phone to take notes? Here's the address."

As Jorge punched the address into his phone, it was almost as if the last nine months hadn't happened.

Almost.

CHAPTER TWO

Sabrina double-checked the dimensions of the school grounds' back wall and decided that she had all the information she needed to file her first report. Knowing Watkins as she did, he would probably have her return later tonight to sneak inside the school and scout a location to stash the bomb, but she wasn't going to do anything without his say-so. Disobedience would get her kicked off this case, and that was something she couldn't afford.

As she made her way back into the flow of people on the sidewalk, she checked the time on her cell phone. She had two hours before she had to file her report. Perfect. That gave her enough time to visit her local contact and set things in motion.

Her contact, Yolanda, worked in a local restaurant and was the only person outside of the *Feiru* Liaison office in Mexico City who knew of Sabrina's true purpose here in Merida. She had made it a habit to eat at the restaurant from her first days on this assignment. Watkins tended to keep an eye on his people, but there was nothing suspicious about going to her favorite restaurant for a late lunch.

Over the last year, Sabrina had passed information over to Yolanda, who would in turn hand it over to Sabrina's boss inside the *Feiru* Liaison section of the Mexican central government. Like all stable governments around the world, certain humans were aware of the existence of the *Feiru* and their first-born children's ability to control the elements. The primary function of the *Feiru* Liaison offices was to prevent worldwide paranoia, no matter the cost.

So far, thanks in large part to the Asylums for Magical Threats prison system, the *Feiru* had kept their elemental magic a secret from the general human population. Sabrina was one of the few privileged humans who knew about the *Feiru*, but she was also part of a growing number of *Feiru* liaison officers who wondered how much longer the secret of elemental magic would last, especially as discord continued to grow between the pro-AMT prison and anti-AMT prison factions amongst the *Feiru*.

And when—not if—the secret got out, Sabrina had no idea what would happen. Humans finding out that magic was real might cause worldwide chaos, or worse, persecution of those deemed "different" from them.

That was why it was imperative she finish this assignment and take down the Fed League. Fringe *Feiru* terrorist groups would only give humans more reason to hate and/or fear the *Feiru*.

She reached the small restaurant a few blocks from the central main plaza and went inside. The hostess greeted her with a smile. After Sabrina sat down at a table near the back of the room, she pretended to look at the menu until Yolanda came up and asked, "Do you want to hear about the specials today or will you have one of your usuals?"

Sabrina looked up at Yolanda. "I think I'll just have my favorite light snack today before I go to work."

Yolanda nodded. A "light snack before work" was code for Sabrina having important information to pass on with the bill. "I'll make sure to put a rush on the order. Did you also want some Chaya juice?"

"Yes, thank you." Sabrina said as she handed the menu over.

The waitress left and Sabrina tried to decide what she'd say in her message. She wanted a team of people she trusted, but getting her boss to agree to that was going to be difficult. Especially since one of those trusted colleagues—Karla Torres—always seemed to be on some kind of probation. But they had worked together on Sabrina's previous assignment and Karla was one of the few people she trusted at her back.

There had been one man inside the Fed League she'd learned to trust nearly as much as Karla, but Sabrina had burned that bridge. It was for the best that she'd never see him again.

Thinking about his humor during their long runs on their days off, or how she'd been determined to beat him at least once in a swimming contest, made her heart ache. She'd always been careful to keep her true self separate from her cover ID, but she'd failed utterly with *him*.

Still, she'd done what she'd had to do to keep him safe. Dwelling on what she wished could've happened would just create more cracks in her delicate psyche. After this assignment was finished, Sabrina was going to take a long vacation and visit her sister down in her home country of Brazil, to re-discover who she truly was.

Her glass of green Chaya juice was placed in front of her and she mumbled her thanks, but the tanned hand around her glass didn't move. She looked up and her heart skipped a beat. She had to be seeing things. There was no way he could be back in Merida, not with the out she'd given him.

But there was no mistaking the long, black hair pulled back from his face, the broad, powerful shoulders, or the scar running through his left eyebrow. The man she'd betrayed all those months ago was back.

She managed to get her voice working again and said, "Why are you here?"

Jorge Salazar sat down in the seat across from her and stared intently with an expression she couldn't read.

~~*

Jorge hadn't known what to expect when he saw Sabrina Ono face-to-face again, but as she stared at him from across the table with her almond-shaped, dark brown eyes, an unexpected mixture of lust and longing shot through his body.

At one time, even just the faintest hint of her scent would've gotten him hard as a rock.

But considering what she'd done to him nine months ago—in addition to the secret he'd learned about her since then—he never would've expected the sight of her smooth skin or her short, sleek black hair tucked behind her ears to send blood to his groin. Shit, he knew it had been a long time, but this was ridiculous. Hadn't he spent months planning his revenge against this woman?

Remembering his imprisonment and sister's torture sobered him up again. He had a job to do. The woman in front of him couldn't be trusted and their past together wouldn't get in the way, no matter what his dick might want.

Jorge raised an eyebrow in nonchalance. "You really want me to answer that here, in a crowded restaurant?"

She whispered, "You shouldn't be here at all."

"That's what you had wanted, wasn't it?" He leaned forward on his arms. "Too bad, because you have information I need, and you fucking owe me. Big time."

Sabrina narrowed her eyes a second before returning to her practiced neutral expression. That was the bitch of working with someone who had the same training as you—they had all the same tricks.

She crossed her arms over her chest, and it took everything he had not to glance down at her breasts as she said, "Stop with the 'I'm such a badass' attitude. Tell me why you're here, and make it quick, unless you want me to call in your little appearance to your former employer."

"You go ahead and do that, backstabber, and I promise you're not going to like what happens next." He swore he saw something flash in her eyes—regret, maybe?—but he quickly brushed it aside. He pushed on. "I told you, I'm here to see you. I saw you scouting that school, and I want all the details."

If she was surprised to learn he'd tailed her, she didn't show it. "You know I can't tell you that."

He studied her for a second and couldn't help but notice the circles under her eyes, or how her cheekbones were more pronounced than the last time he'd seen her. She clearly wasn't taking care of herself. For a second, he wondered what was going on in her life, but then he clenched his fist and told himself that he didn't care. No, make that he couldn't care.

Remember, you need to succeed in order to protect Alejandra.

He leaned back in his chair. "Well, I'm not leaving you alone until you agree to answer some questions. We can either do it here, in full view of whoever might be watching. Or, I can go wait outside and you can wait a few minutes before joining me. Which way will it be, Ms. Saito?"

Sabrina tensed a second and Jorge knew he had her. She recovered quickly and whispered, "What did you call me?"

"Oh, I think you heard the first time. So, unless you want me to share your little secret with your superiors, you're going to answer my questions."

~~*

Sabrina was having a hard time keeping herself together. Jorge was good at reading people, and she didn't want to give him any more fodder to use against her than was necessary. If she'd heard him correctly, she had a huge problem on her hands.

Saito was the alias last name she had used in her previous assignment down in Rio de Janeiro. How in the hell had he found out about it? And if he knew that, what else did he know?

Suddenly, the optimism she'd had about finishing this assignment and getting the hell out of Merida vanished. One word about using an alias, and her Fed League superiors—including Watkins—would toss her into a cold, dark room and torture the truth out of her. While she'd been trained to resist spilling secrets under torture, she had no desire to test it.

Everything she'd worked for, and all the deaths she'd caused over the last two years would be for nothing if Jorge made one call and shared her secret.

Focus. It was useless to start obsessing over anything until she had more information. The only way she was going to get that was getting Salazar to talk.

She gave him a cool look. "I'll talk, but not here. I'm not promising you anything in terms of answers, but I'll give you five minutes."

"Fine, I'll meet you outside. But if you try to sneak out the back or try to give me the slip, I'll still find you and I won't be so nice the next time. Considering what you did, I'm sure you'd agree that I've been pretty fucking restrained."

At the mention of her betrayal, guilt started to nibble at her. But she pushed it aside and looked down her nose at him. "Nine months might have passed, but I haven't forgotten about your tracking skills."

He pushed back his chair from the table. "Good. I'll be waiting for you outside."

"Where?"

"Don't worry. I'll find you."

His words held an underlying threat, but it was his intense gaze that made her heart rate kick up. Whatever had happened to him in the last nine months, it hadn't been good. Jorge Salazar was no longer the easygoing young man with a sense of humor and a passion for making things right. He was angrier, more serious, and more mature. She wondered what had happened to him.

That question was on the tip of her tongue, but she held back. Until she found out what he knew, she needed to be careful.

Jorge turned and left without another word, and she released a breath. The possibility of him knowing she was an undercover *Feiru* Liaison officer was bad enough, but being seen with Jorge Salazar in public wasn't much better.

His picture was on the list of former Fed League members to avoid at all costs. If they were seen together, Watkins or one of her other superiors might suspect she was either working with someone else or thinking about leaving. Hopefully, she'd kicked Jorge out of the restaurant quick enough to avoid attracting notice.

She needed to get out of here. The sooner she found out what Jorge knew, the sooner she could think of a way to get rid of him. She couldn't turn him in to their superiors as she'd done last time, right after she'd seen his arm turn into a shadowy mist. Maybe once she had talked with him a little, she could think of a new plan.

Yolanda returned with her order and Sabrina realized she couldn't leave until she finished what she'd come to do. "I'm sorry, but something came up. Can I get the check?"

Yolanda stopped short of frowning before she nodded and left again. No doubt she'd seen the strange man, but Sabrina had never brought Jorge here, even when they had been friends. Yolanda would probably just dismiss him as part of her current assignment.

Once Yolanda had brought the check, Sabrina scrawled her coded message on the back, requesting a meet-up with her boss tomorrow at their usual market. She handed the bill to her and smiled. "Thank you."

"Anytime."

Sabrina exited the restaurant, keeping her eyes and ears open. While she didn't see Jorge anywhere, she was confident he'd find her. She turned right and started walking.

The further she went from the restaurant, the more irritated she became. She had less than an hour before she had to file her first report, and she couldn't give Watkins any reason to dismiss her from the school job.

Just as she pulled out her cell phone to check the time again, a hand grabbed her and covered her mouth before pulling her down the empty street. Sabrina knew better than to scream, especially since the man's touch and scent were familiar.

Jorge Salazar had found her.

Chapter Three

As Jorge dragged Sabrina further down the abandoned street, away from prying eyes, he tried not to notice how his arm kept brushing the underside of her breasts. The friction of her ass brushing against his cock wasn't much better. And then there was her scent—a mixture of vanilla and woman that he'd never quite forgotten.

Damn it, as much as he didn't need her to know how much her scent and touch still affected him, his dick was sending out rocket flares—I'm here, I'm hard, and I want you.

He reached the large van he'd been aiming for and slid in between the six-foot high van and the nondescript sedan behind him. He managed to turn Sabrina around so that her back was now against the van, and he placed one arm across her shoulders and the other still covering her mouth. While their bodies weren't touching as much as when he'd been dragging her, she was still far too close. The sooner he got the information he needed from her, the better.

Her eyes stared into his without fear as he said, "If I remove my hand and you scream, you're not going to like it. Understand?"

She nodded, and the instant he let go, she said, "Whatever you're trying to prove, it's unnecessary. I have an appointment I need to keep, so cut straight to the point."

So much for soft words. She was treating him like the enemy. Good, that would make things easier.

He leaned in and took satisfaction in the slight widening of her eyes. Okay, maybe she wasn't as unaffected by him as he'd originally thought. That was something else he could use against her. "I want to know what Watkins has planned for that elementary school." She opened her mouth, but he beat her to it. "And before you say you can't do it, just remember I know about your other identity, down in Brazil, and I'll blackmail you if that's what it takes."

"Isn't that what you're doing right now?"

He gave a half-smile. "Well, then you'd better start talking, Sabrina—if that's even your real name."

She pushed against his chest. "It is asshole. But even with your blackmail threats, I won't tell you anything until you let me know what you plan to do with the information."

He narrowed his eyes. "Why? Did you develop soft feelings for Watkins and the others in my absence? After all, you're good at that, charming people into believing you're their friend."

She growled and tried to push him away, but he kept his arm in place. She said, "Fine. Get out your hatred. You don't know all the facts, but feel free to jump to conclusions. Just make all your witty comments and accusations quick, because I am leaving in the next five minutes, whether you approve of it or not."

~~*

Sabrina knew she should keep her temper in check, but she decided to screw it. If Jorge was going to be an asshole, she wasn't going to play nice.

22

SHADOW OF TEMPTATION

To be honest, if she didn't have a deadline hanging over her head, she probably would've tried to reason with him and have an actual conversation. But as much as she didn't want Jorge to hate her for the wrong reasons, her mission was too important. There was no way she was going to let down her boss in Mexico City or those innocent schoolchildren.

Of course, the question was how she was going to carry out the threat she'd just issued. Jorge had always been strong—a result of their frequent runs and swims—but the defined muscles of his arms were new. She would never be able to overpower him.

Then she remembered the feel of his erection against her ass and had an idea. She'd always known that Jorge had had a thing for her. She'd ignored it in the past because A) she was undercover and B) he'd been too bright-eyed and optimistic for her to dare bring him into the shady areas of her life.

But now that she knew her betrayal hadn't affected his attraction, she'd use it against him if she had to.

Jorge was still staring at her in silence. She was about to repeat her question when he said, "I need information about Watkins to protect my sister Alejandra."

She blinked. That was the last thing she'd expected to hear. "What are you talking about?"

He searched her eyes a second, and then leaned close. She could feel the heat of his breath against her cheek as he whispered, "Don't play dumb. You're the one who turned me in. The Collector pays handsomely for strange abilities like mine. If you had done your research, then you'd know the extent of what that bitch does to further her own goals."

Sabrina was completely lost. "I have no idea what you're talking about. I turned you in to our superior to get you kicked out of the Fed League. That's it. This is the first I've ever heard of anyone known as the 'Collector'."

She saw him hesitate a second, and then he shook his head. "Enough with the lies. Unless you want my sister to be tortured again, and most likely killed this time, you need to start talking. I don't give a fuck about your appointment. You're not leaving until I say so."

~~*

Deep down, Jorge knew being an asshole was not the best way to get information out of someone. But his time with the Collector had erased any vestiges of patience and tact he'd once had.

Just remembering his sister's chattering and cries for help— the Collector's people had locked Alejandra naked in a freezer and broadcast her agony into his locked cell—made him even more pissed off. Sabrina, the woman he'd tricked himself into believing he loved, was responsible for Alejandra's suffering as well as his own.

Still, the look of horror in Sabrina's eyes as he told her about his sister almost appeared genuine. Had she really not known what spilling one man's secret could do?

No. He wasn't going to let an old soft spot for this woman fuck with his head. "Well, Sabrina, say something."

She opened her mouth and then closed it. He tightened his grip on her shoulder and she finally spoke up. "I don't know who the hell you are anymore, Salazar. Even if I told you what I know, what guarantee do I have that you won't kill me?"

He resisted a blink. "You think I'd kill you?"

"Considering how you're hurting me right now, it's certainly crossed my mind."

Realizing the truth, he relaxed his grip a fraction. He wasn't going to turn into the killer the Collector had tried to mold him to be, not even with this woman. "I won't kill you. You're more valuable alive."

She poked a finger into his chest. "As much as I'd like to believe your little heartfelt promise, I'm going to need something more. Let's make a deal."

"A deal? I think I have the upper hand right now, princess. So stop stalling. I know you're trying to think of a way to escape."

She lowered her hand from his chest and let out a noise of frustration. "You want the truth? Then listen up, because I'm only going to say this once: I need to file a report with Watkins in the next forty minutes or he'll throw me off the case. If that happens, we'll both be fucked."

His curiosity got the better of him and he asked, "What do you mean 'we'll both be fucked'? Does this have anything to do with you using another name?"

She raised her chin a notch. "Let me file my report, and I'll answer more of your questions."

"What guarantee do I have that you won't backstab me later?"

"Believe nothing else about me, but I always told the truth about my mother. I swear on her grave that I won't betray you unless you give me a reason to do so."

Memories of Sabrina's tears as she told him about her mother's death flashed into his head. That had been the moment he'd started to fall for the woman he thought was Sabrina Ono. Had it been part of her ruse or had her tears been genuine?

More than likely, this was a trick. But he couldn't risk losing the only lead he had on Watkins. "Fine. But I'm coming with you to watch you file your report. That's my condition."

~~*

Sabrina relaxed her hand and lowered it down from Jorge's crotch. If he hadn't agreed to her deal, she would've grabbed his balls and twisted. Making the bitter man angry was not the smartest idea, but it'd been all she had.

Luckily, he'd agreed. "All right then, let me go so we can get moving."

"Until we get to wherever it is we're going, I'm going to hold your hand the entire way." He took her right hand—her dominant one, of course—and squeezed. "If you don't want to attract attention, then you'd better act like my girlfriend."

She tried to pull away—this would most certainly get her caught if anyone was following her—but all he did in response was to pull her close against his side and say, "If you stay close and act like you adore me, people are less likely to pay attention to you. So, are you ready?"

She glared and tried her best to ignore the heat radiating off Jorge's body. She hated to admit it, but Jorge was physically stronger than her. She'd never get free until either he allowed it, or she found a weapon to help even the odds.

Her best option was to use side streets and back alleys to avoid running into any of her Fed League colleagues. The plan wasn't foolproof, but it was the best she could do for now.

She squeezed his hand back, careful to dig her nails into his skin. To his credit, he didn't even flinch.

She finally answered him. "Your plan is pretty shitty—and will probably get us both caught—but it's not like I have a choice."

He shrugged. "Hey, things could be a lot worse, princess."

"Stop calling me princess."

"I would think it wouldn't matter, seeing as you use different names in different places."

She grit her teeth. She wasn't going to argue any further. The more she argued, the more likely she would spill secrets she couldn't afford to spill. Why she wanted him to believe her, she didn't know. He'd made his hatred of her clear.

Instead, she focused on keeping up their farce and maneuvering them through the streets to her apartment. But when Jorge adjusted his hand to get a better grip, she couldn't ignore how she liked the way his rough skin felt against hers. Then he brushed his thumb over the back of her hand, and Sabrina drew in a breath at his light touch.

What the hell? The man hated her and clearly wanted nothing to do with her, so why was she so aware of him? She had succeeded in ignoring his advances for nearly a year. She should be able to keep doing it.

Then the image of him back at the van, mere inches from her face, his gaze intent, sent a thrill through her body. This new version of Jorge could take the shady dealings of her life—and more.

Cut it out, Sabrina. Just because the fiercer new version of Jorge did things to her insides, and lower, didn't mean she could act on them. Right now, she needed to file her report and then brace herself for another onslaught of Jorge-the-distrustful-asshole.

Her top priority was finding out how much he knew about her past.

They soon arrived at her apartment and she fumbled in her attempt to get her keys out of her pocket. She looked up at Jorge. "If I have to try and unlock my door with my left hand, we'll be here all night."

He let go and she instantly felt the loss of his heat. She ignored it, took out her keys, and unlocked the door. She motioned for him to enter, but he shook his head and said, "After you."

Smart move, as she had some booby traps in place. She inched the door open and unhooked the string trigger before swinging the door wide open. She had no qualms about Jorge being here since she kept no personal information in her apartment, but she'd developed a slight sense of paranoia from her time tracking down a *Feiru* counterfeiter back in Brazil. These days, she always wanted to know if someone had entered her apartment in her absence.

She flipped on the light and saw everything was untouched, so she walked inside and made a beeline for her laptop. Just as she'd expected, Jorge entered behind her and shut the door.

She waved toward the kitchen. "Make yourself something to eat, if you like. This is going to take me about ten minutes."

Instead of going to the kitchen or even sitting down on the couch, he moved to stand behind her. "No, I think I'm going to stay here and watch over your shoulder."

She shrugged, wanting to show she wasn't intimidated by his proximity. "Fine. The report I'm about to type isn't anything you couldn't find out yourself."

He remained silent, but he was standing close enough she could feel his heat behind her. *Ignore it, Sabrina.* She'd been around hot men before without drooling all over herself. She could certainly do it now, when both her career and a school of children were at stake.

With the safety of the children in mind, she started typing her report.

Chapter Four

Jorge read Sabrina's email to Watkins as she typed. It was all about school dimensions, weak points, and when the cleaning staff arrived and left. She'd been right—all of this he could have found out with half a day's stakeout.

None of it was the key to taking down Watkins. Only the woman sitting in front of him could do that.

As he waited for her to finish typing, his gaze settled on the skin of her neck. The last time he'd seen her, Sabrina's hair had been a few inches past her shoulders. He wondered if the change of appearance was a sign of her about to switch identities again.

He tried to use her lying to him to stoke his anger, but it wasn't working as well as it had in the restaurant or back at the van.

Taking her hand and holding it the whole way here had been a mistake. He'd done it to make sure she didn't run away, but all it had succeeded in doing was reminding him how soft and delicate her hand felt in his.

Of course, describing Sabrina whatever-her-name as delicate was ridiculous. The woman could run ten miles and still breathe easy; she was even stronger in the water. Not to mention she could take down men nearly twice her size with nothing but a few quick self-defense moves.

Yet despite all of that, standing right behind her, her vanilla and womanly scent filled his nose and he couldn't help but notice her as a woman. Memories of her vanilla scent had both tortured him over the last nine months as well as focused him. Being chained to a bed and pumped full of drugs to keep from shifting had become routine during his time with the Collector. Thinking of how to get back at Sabrina had kept him from going insane, or worse, turning into a sociopathic killer.

Yet here she was, right in front of him, and revenge was the furthest thing from his mind. His semi-hard cock was proof that while his head understood what Sabrina had done, his dick did not.

Luckily, Sabrina closed her laptop and turned around. Good. He could finally get down to business. The sooner he finished this, the sooner he could leave this woman and never have to see her again.

Sabrina stood up. "I'm done. I should receive a follow-up email in the next half-hour, so start talking because I'm kicking you out as soon as I hear the little buzzing on my phone that signals Watkins's response."

To put distance between them, he stepped back and crossed his arms over his chest. "As much as I'm glad you're submitting so easily, I feel there's a catch."

She rolled her eyes. "I resist, and you bitch. Then I cooperate, and you bitch some more. I don't know what happened to you, but clearly it erased any sort of manners you once had."

"That's right, princess. And let's not forget who's ultimately responsible for that."

"Right. Me." She waved an arm and moved to the kitchen. "Have at it. Call me names and blame me some more. But if you don't mind, some grumpy, angry man interrupted my meal, so I'm going to make something to eat while you do it."

She opened the fridge and Jorge narrowed his eyes. Unlike his other targets in the last few months, Sabrina wasn't afraid of him. She probably remembered the kinder, somewhat shy version he'd once been.

Well, he needed to fix that because that young man was dead.

He was across the room with a few strides. Grabbing her shoulder, he turned her around so her ass was against the counter. He switched his grip to her wrists and pinned her legs with his own to prevent her from trying to escape. "Listen, Sabrina the Mystery Woman. This is not a game. You know as well as I that the clock is ticking. I need you to tell me why you don't want to get kicked off this assignment for Watkins, and then start spilling everything you know."

~~*

Sabrina was not only hungry, but also irritated with both herself and Jorge. The fact he now had her pinned in place didn't help her mood.

But her irritation was stronger than her hormones, and she barely noticed his heat surrounding her. Right now, all she wanted to do was scream that she was an undercover agent. Maybe then he'd shut up. Of course, she couldn't do that. Any human working for one of the *Feiru* Liaison offices who exposed their employer would be pulled from the field and usually stashed away for life. She didn't know where—nobody did—but call her selfish for not wanting someone to make her disappear.

SHADOW OF TEMPTATION

She tried to wiggle free, but just as she expected, it was hopeless. The only way to get free was for Jorge to release her. For once, she wished she wasn't human but rather a first-born *Feiru* with magic at her disposal. Then she'd be able to teach him a lesson about manhandling someone against their will.

But no, she didn't have any magic. All she could do was answer his questions and stick as close to the truth as possible without revealing her secrets. "First, despite whatever you might think, I do have a heart and I'm not about to let a school full of children be blown up for who the hell knows what reason."

He frowned. "So you don't know why Watkins is targeting this school?"

The Fed League's usual M.O. was to target AMT-related people or former employees. As far as she knew, the school didn't employ any former AMT employees. The parents of the school's students didn't check out either.

She shook her head. "No. I have no idea why the school was chosen."

He looked skeptical but thankfully didn't push. "You said 'first'. So, what's the other reason?"

Of course he'd catch that. Her next words could be dangerous, but a new idea made her want to chance it. If she could get a Shadow-Shifter to work with her, sneaking into Watkins's rooms would be a breeze. "Second, I want to take down Watkins just as much as you do."

She watched Jorge's face closely. She couldn't read any reaction, but she knew what was coming.

Jorge raised his eyebrows. "How convenient that you also want to take down Watkins. What's the reason?"

She raised her chin. "I want to leave the Fed League, but I'll never be able to do that as long as Watkins is around."

"Why now? It took a lot of digging for me to learn about your other identity. No doubt you could pull the same stunt again, and disappear without getting caught."

Time to make up some believable excuses. "I don't have the same resources as before. The only way for me to leave is to take out the man holding the Fed League together. Watkins is the only one who takes this organization's aim seriously, and only because he's paid to. The other so-called leaders just bicker and have petty arguments, each trying to outrank the other and prove they have the biggest dick. Lock away their leader and the Fed League goes back into obscurity." She moved her head closer to his. "You don't like me, that's clear. But agree to work with me, and I'll help you bring down Harry Watkins in a matter of days."

~~*

Jorge couldn't tell from Sabrina's body language if she were telling the truth or not. However, all of this seemed a little too convenient for his liking.

Before he'd been kicked out, he and Sabrina had been close. Going on long runs together, racing in the pool, or even sharing a quiet moment sitting on a park bench—they'd spent nearly every free moment together. Jorge had done it because he'd been infatuated with the spirited woman. Now, however, he was starting to wonder why Sabrina had hung around with him in the first place. He hadn't had any special protections or friends in high places. He'd just been an angry young man swayed by promises of revenge. Being surrounded by people who'd also had family members tortured and abused inside the AMT had made him feel at home.

Yet Sabrina had always sought out his company, even after she'd turned down his advances for more. Hell, he'd tried to kiss her more than once.

But never had she mentioned wanting to get out of the Fed League. Nor had she shown any dislike of Harry Watkins beyond the usual discontent of the Fed League recruits.

True, something could've happened to her between then and now, but his gut told him something else was going on. "Let's pretend what you've told me is true. What's your plan for taking down Watkins? What happens next?"

A buzzing sound came from near the laptop, where Sabrina had put her phone. She glanced over and then tried to push him away, but Jorge didn't budge. She frowned up at him and said, "I need to check and see if that's Watkins."

He shook his head. "I'm not about to waste time pinning you up against the counter again to get a clear answer. Tell me what you have planned; then I'll let you check your message."

She held his gaze for a few seconds before sighing. "I'm in the process of finding people to help me break into his rooms and hopefully take him down."

He hadn't expected an answer. "Yeah, and how exactly are you going to make that happen?"

She shook her head. "No, this isn't a case of me spilling my plans with nothing in return." She tried to get free of his grip, but failed. "Before I tell you anything else, you're going to tell me how taking down Watkins will protect your sister."

Damn, she'd remembered about that. But this was his chance to make Sabrina really understand what she'd done nine months ago.

"Fine." He leaned in close so she would have to look into his eyes. "I refused to use my shadow-shifting abilities to kill. The

35

Collector didn't like it, and she brought in my sister to change my mind."

Jorge kept a tight rein on his emotions. The next few sentences weren't going to be easy, but Sabrina needed to understand the enormity of what had happened to Alejandra. "They usually chained me up and tranquilized me to keep from shifting. Rather than risk me being lucid and torturing Alejandra in front of me, they decided to take their cruelty up another notch."

Usually he kept the memories locked up tight, but this time he let them out. He continued, "At first, I thought they were just playing random sounds of a woman calling for help. She kept chattering because of the cold, her words getting fainter as time went on. But once sounds of slapping started, the woman started crying and begging for 'Jorge to help her.' The more she talked about our past, the more I started to realize—even through my drug-haze—they had Alejandra."

His sister had already told him she forgave him in the brief video he'd seen of her after she'd been rescued by DEFEND, and that she still loved him. But he had no idea how he was going to face her. Not just because of what had happened to her, but also because of what he'd had to do to stop her torture.

"Jorge." He looked up and wished he hadn't. Sabrina's face was soft, her eyes kind. He released her wrists and tried to step back, but Sabrina grabbed the front of his shirt and said, "I'm sorry for what happened to your sister."

He succeeded in breaking her grip and took a few steps away from her. "Don't you see? If you had just talked to me instead of going behind my back, none of that would've happened."

Shadow of Temptation

~~*

While working for the *Feiru* Liaison office, Sabrina's actions had caused pain, torture, and even death in the past. Somehow she'd found a way to carry on and do her job. But this time, with a man she'd once called friend, she wasn't able to push away her guilt.

"I—" She took a deep breath. She needed to make him understand her actions, too. "I did it because I wanted you to move on to better things. You always talked about bigger and better plans to help the first-borns, but I knew you wouldn't leave unless I did. And I couldn't leave."

Jorge looked skeptical. "Your vague statements aren't helping your case. If you want me to even remotely start to believe you, I need a hell of a lot more information than that."

In that instant, she wanted to tell him everything. About her secret identities and her training. About her true reasons for joining the Fed League. About how close she was to cracking because of the strain of living a lie for too long.

Her life didn't lend itself to many friends, but despite whatever had happened between her and Jorge, he had been her friend once. Could she trust him?

He was the key to finishing this assignment quickly. His abilities would lessen the risk of exposure or danger to herself or others. She couldn't tell him the full truth, but half-truths might just work.

Of course, he'd get suspicious if she made it too easy for him. She folded her arms over her chest. "I'll spill some details if you promise me that you won't maliciously use them against me." He opened his mouth, but she cut him off. "I know, I turned you in, but my reasons were to do what was best for you, not to cause you harm."

He stared at her, and she stared back. Finally, he said, "As long as you hold up a promise to keep my shadow-shifting abilities secret and not tell anyone you've seen me, then I'll consider it."

"Just like that, you're going to believe me?"

He shook his head. "I didn't say I was going to believe you, but the sooner I get this damn mission done, the sooner I can leave and never have to deal with you again. I'll agree to most anything to make that happen."

His words shouldn't hurt—after all, she had wanted him to forget about her—but they did. Seeing Jorge had given her a small glimpse of her past, and had reminded her that she was not just an undercover agent, but also a person with her own likes and dislikes. More than anything, she wanted to have friends again.

She barely prevented herself from starting at that dangerous line of thinking. Sabrina 'the person' didn't matter during an undercover mission. Only success mattered.

Still, she hoped that something of the old Jorge was still around and he wouldn't betray her at the first opportunity. Torture made people unpredictable, and while Jorge had only mentioned being restrained and drugged, she had a feeling there was more to it.

Her best bet was to keep her concerns and hurt to herself, so she said, "Then we both agree finishing this ASAP is all that matters." He nodded and she added, "Then I'll start being clearer. At the time I turned you in, I knew how you felt about me, Jorge. It was a distraction to both you and me, so I need to find a way to get rid of you. Getting you kicked out had seemed like the best thing at the time, but I am truly sorry for the events that happened afterward. I had never intended for you, let alone your sister, to go through such hell because of one five minute meeting with our old superior. If I'd known he would sell you out to the crazy Collector lady, I never would've betrayed you."

She'd expected some kind of anger or demand of explanation, but he surprised her when he asked, "Why can't you leave the Fed League?"

This was going to be dangerously close to admitting the truth, but fuck it. Nothing else would work. "Because I only joined the Fed League in order to find a way to take it down."

Chapter Five

Jorge had expected Sabrina to say something along the lines of, "They'd threatened to hurt so-and-so if I didn't stay." The Fed League had something in common with the Collector—they both tended to use people against you to get what they wanted.

Instead, she'd blindsided him and he couldn't help but blink. "What?"

Sabrina raised her chin. "I know it sounds crazy, but you worked with me long enough to know that I'm good at collecting information."

"Gathering information is one thing, but single-handedly taking down a semi-crazy organization is another. What were you going to do, charm your way to the top and assassinate someone? Fucking hell, Sabrina. That's just naive and stupid."

Her eyes flashed. "Gee, and you wonder why I never told you?"

He narrowed his eyes. "Hold on a second. We talked all the time *before*. And old Jorge was a whole fucking lot nicer than I am. I'm starting to wonder if we were friends at all."

As soon as the words left his mouth, Jorge wanted to take them back. He was supposed to hate Sabrina Ono, so why did he care if any of it had been real.

Because, asshole, deep down you're starting to believe she didn't turn you in to the Collector on purpose.

No. Screw that. He had a mission to finish before the Collector's people found him. The longer he argued with Sabrina, the more time he gave them to track him down.

Then Sabrina did something he should've expected, but had overlooked, and she bolted toward her cell phone.

"Shit." He went after her, but she had the phone before he could tackle her to the ground. They rolled, but Jorge managed to pin her through a combination of securing her legs to the ground with his weight and holding her wrists up above her head.

She wriggled and tried to throw him off, but it wasn't working and he was too angry to let his dick take control of the situation. Instead, he focused on his irritation with both Sabrina and himself. "I know your escape tricks, princess. I tried to be nice and gave you time to explain things, but now we're going to do it my way."

She moved again, but it was still useless. Her angry eyes bored into his. "What? Are you going to yell at me some more?"

"No. I have something a hell of a lot more fun in mind."

~~*

Harry Watkins scanned Sabrina Ono's report and then put down his phone. How he would respond depended on what information he could get out of the woman currently strapped to the metal table in front of him.

He had had one of his people follow Sabrina to the restaurant. Normally, he wouldn't think twice about Ono, but the elementary school plan needed to go off without a hitch or his rival—Luis Gomez—would never stop poaching the *Feiru* with latent abilities in the area. Watkins was this close to claiming the whole Yucatan peninsula as his territory.

41

He took the woman's wet chin and forced her to look up at him. "Are you ready to tell me why Sabrina Ono was seen with that man at your restaurant, or do you need some more convincing?"

The woman named Yolanda looked from him to the man standing above her with a wet cloth and back again. "I-I don't know anything. She's just a regular customer. I know her name is Sabrina Ono and that she really likes Chaya juice, but that's it, I swear."

He released her chin, signaled to the blonde woman standing on the far side of the room, and she came over. He took the paper from her hands and lowered it to the waitress's face. "The back of this receipt is written in code. I have my people working on it. I suggest that you cooperate now, or you're not going to like what happens when I find out the truth later."

The woman had on a strong face, but her voice wavered as she said, "How can I tell you what I don't know?"

This was getting him nowhere. The easiest way to get the human talking would be to use the special "soldier" the Collector had lent him. The blonde female Siren could sing a command and the human wouldn't be able to resist; she'd be telling all of her secrets within seconds.

But the Siren had to rest her abilities between uses or risk losing her voice forever. Watkins would rather save her skills for something more important.

Instead, he nodded to his man standing above the woman's head and said, "Again."

The man lowered the cloth over the woman's face and another man brought over a bucket of water. Once the man started pouring, he ignored the waitress's struggles and turned toward the Siren. "Tell your mistress I'm going to need more soldiers, preferably ones that can help me capture someone with at least half a brain."

The Siren nodded and exited the room. The Collector was as anxious as he to get rid of Luis Gomez. With him gone, she would have full access to the latent abilities in the area to fill out her army. Not only would it make the bitch happy, it would make Watkins a very rich and powerful man.

He turned back toward the waitress and signaled for his people to stop waterboarding her. Once the wet cloth was removed from Yolanda's face, she started sputtering. He waited a second to avoid getting spit on before he leaned down, grabbed her hair, and yanked. Hard. "Last chance. Tell me what you know about Sabrina Ono and the coded message, or the next time I'll let you drown."

The woman shook her head. "I-I don't have anything new to tell you."

He released her hair and leaned back. He looked to his men. "Do what you will with her before you kill her. Report to me what you find afterward."

The man nodded and Watkins turned away. Maybe once the men had raped her and cut her up a bit, she would start talking.

$*\sim*\sim*$

Sabrina tugged on the cloth restraints tied around her wrists and legs, but they held firm. The restraints were tied to the metal frame holding up the bed. She might be able to get free if she had a few hours, but she needed to get free as soon as possible. Jorge had taken her phone and read her message. Yet the bastard hadn't shared what the message had contained. If she didn't reply soon, everything would be compromised.

True, things could be a lot worse. At least she was still alive.

Jorge had changed more than she'd thought. She started to believe what he'd said about the kinder, shyer version of Jorge Salazar being dead. He took what he wanted, didn't hesitate, and was more straightforward than she'd ever hope to be. The drastic changes should make it easier to distance herself from him and use him as a tool.

But deep down, in a place she barely wanted to admit existed, she kind of liked the changes in him.

Between her time in Rio and here in Merida, she'd had to keep her head down and blend in or risk being discovered. After three years, however, she was getting tired of having to hide what she thought remained of her true personality.

Jorge might be frustrating as hell—and more than a little bit of an asshole—but it'd felt good to get angry and even dish out a few sarcastic quips. He would be able to handle anything she threw his way. Considering she'd irritated the hell out of her sister and parents with her tendency to argue and talk back as a child, standing up to her was quite an achievement.

The noise of shuffling furniture and random objects stopped and Sabrina watched the door. Sure enough, Jorge appeared and leaned against the doorjamb. "Well, at least you're a smart one. I didn't find anything remotely personal in the apartment." He held up her cell phone. "The only real information I could find was on here."

Remember, showing your anger will only make things worse. She took a calming breath and acted as if nothing were out of the ordinary. That should annoy Jorge. "And when do you plan on sharing that information with me?" She darted a glance to her restraints and back to his face. "I can't do anything if Watkins sends a reply and I don't answer."

He moved to stand beside the bed and looked down at her. From her supine position, it was impossible to miss the strength in his shoulders or the determined look in his eye. This version of Jorge could be dangerous.

"The message wasn't from Watkins, but some guy named Miguel."

Okay, she hadn't expected that answer. Miguel was her contact Yolanda's boss. "What did he want?"

He sat on the edge of the bed and his knee brushed against her side. She nearly jumped at the touch—in a good way. Jorge didn't seem to have noticed the way his casual touch branded her skin, and that irritated her. Why should his touch affect her and not him? She definitely didn't need the distraction.

He brushed her with his leg again and it took everything she had to remain still as he answered, "Yolanda never came back from her break, and he was wondering if you knew where she was."

Dread started to pool in the pit of her stomach. Yolanda's disappearance was probably related in some way to Sabrina or her work. "Did he say anything else?"

He shook his head. "No. What aren't you telling me?"

Time to stick close to the truth without giving it. "Yolanda was helping me with some information. The fact she disappeared right after you showed up tells me that someone saw us together, and my entire participation in Watkins's assignment might be compromised." She tugged on the restraints. "I need you to free me so I can try to salvage this situation. If Yolanda gets hurt because of your stupid-ass move, then I will never forgive you."

"So now you have other people working with you?" He leaned down until his face was only a few inches from hers. "You're still keeping something from me. Save us both some time and start talking."

She growled. Screw liking this version of Jorge. "No. I'm not going to risk my friend's life by wasting my time arguing with you. Let me go."

Jorge leaned back and stood up. "No. I think you need some time to cool off and reconsider telling me what you know."

He walked to the door and Sabrina started to feel a sense of panic. "Jorge Salazar, let me go! Whatever may have happened to you, I never would've guessed that you'd let someone die just to further your own goals."

He stopped when he reached the doorway and looked over his shoulder. "I'll look into your friend's disappearance. I still have contacts in the area who can help."

She blinked. "What?"

"Nice to see how you really think of me, but I'm not a cold-hearted bastard. Just a determined one."

He took a step out of the room and she said, "Wait, you aren't seriously going to leave me tied up here, are you?"

He shrugged his shoulders. "Why not? But don't get too comfy. We'll be moving locations in a few hours."

With that, he left her.

~~*

Jorge went into the bathroom and shut the door to get some privacy. Sure, he needed to make some calls and check on Sabrina's friend, but he also needed to work on killing his erection.

SHADOW OF TEMPTATION

He'd never really thought about tying a woman to a bed before, but the image of Sabrina tied up and vulnerable had sent blood rushing to his cock. That woman had gotten one thing right—he was different from the man she'd known before.

Hell, before his time with the Collector, he'd barely had enough nerve to try to kiss Sabrina. Now he imagined taking her tied up on the bed.

Think of something else. If he'd had any chance at all with Sabrina, it was gone now. Especially as he was going to have to treat her more as a prisoner until either she worked with him willingly or they succeeded in capturing Watkins.

That thought kicked his head back into the game. He took out the brand new burner phone he'd brought with him and punched in his DEFEND contact's number. The phone rang once before a woman answered, "Yes?"

"Santos, I need you to check a few things out for me."

"Have you gotten anywhere with your assignment?"

"Nearly. I've tapped a few people I used to know, but one person has gone missing. I need you to check on a waitress named Yolanda from Cafe Maya. She's disappeared, and I think it might be because of me."

"You don't even have a last name or address for me? I have other things to do, Salazar. Unless you can give me a concrete reason why you need to find this woman, I'm going to pass."

Jorge clenched the phone. DEFEND had assigned Isabel Santos as his contact here in Merida, but the woman never made things easy. "I've got the Collector's people to deal with, on top of being a wanted ex-Fed League member, and don't have time for your complaints. If you have any issues, take it up with your leaders. Aislinn is the one who ordered you to help me in any way that you can."

Aislinn was one of the co-leaders of DEFEND. Jorge might have only had a few phone conversations with the woman, but even he knew you did what she ordered, no questions asked. Santos, who'd worked for DEFEND for years, knew that even better than he did.

The line went silent for a few seconds. When Santos finally replied, her tone was unnaturally even. "Fine. Let's say I find out information on this waitress. How can I contact you?"

"I have another cell phone I haven't used and keep for emergencies. Here's the number." He gave it and then said, "One last thing. I need a safe house to use."

"Demanding one, aren't you?"

"Cut the shit. Just give me an address and tell me where to find the key."

"Fine, dickwad. You ready?"

"Yes, sunshine, get on with it."

He jotted down the information and hung up the phone before taking out the battery and tossing it on the ground. After smashing the phone with his boot, he ran his fingers through his hair and decided what to do next. Normally, he'd knock someone unconscious or use his shadow-shifting skills to transport a captive to a new location. Right now, however, he couldn't do the latter because his powers hadn't recharged yet, and Jorge had no wish to die trying to use them again before the twenty-four hour mark.

The former he didn't want to do because of his fucking conscience. How that bastard had survived, Jorge didn't know, but he'd already tied Sabrina up. He didn't want to see how much more uncooperative she'd become if he knocked her out.

But why should he care? Getting her to hate him more would make it easier to force her away once this was over. As long as her friend was possibly missing and those schoolchildren were still in danger, she'd do whatever it took to make both situations right—even if it meant working with him.

Jorge reached into one of the pockets of his BDU pants and took out the little assassin-slash-spy kit he always carried. He flipped it open, grabbed the small needle and bottle of drugs, and laid the case aside. As he filled the syringe with the clear liquid, he had a split-second flash of regret, but then he pushed that motherfucker aside and headed for the room holding Sabrina.

Chapter Six

Sabrina slowly opened her eyes, but the brightness made it feel like a thousand tiny needles were poking her eyeballs, so she promptly shut them again. What the hell? What would cause the light to hurt like that?

After about a minute, she tried to open her eyes again. This time she kept them open long enough to notice the pale blue color of the walls. This wasn't her apartment, which meant Jorge must've moved them.

She closed her eyes again and tried to remember the last thing that had happened to her. Then it hit her—she remembered Jorge-the-asshole pricking her with a needle, and then nothing. Now forcing her eyes to remain open long enough to look around, she could see she was in a small bedroom with faded pictures on the walls and a small en suite bathroom off to the side. Her best guess was that this was a cheap hotel or a low-budget hostel room.

Her training prevented her from freaking out at waking up in a strange place. She'd been fortunate in the past and hadn't yet experienced being drugged outside of her training days with the *Feiru* Liaison office down in Brazil. The feeling was unpleasant, like someone was banging a drum inside her head, but she'd live.

She was more concerned about the meeting with her boss from the Mexico City *Feiru* Liaison office. She had no way of knowing if Yolanda had succeeded in passing on the message before she went missing.

Yolanda. She didn't know a whole lot about the woman's private life, but she'd been putting herself in danger to help Sabrina for nearly a year. If something happened to her, it would be Sabrina's fault.

She clenched her fists and decided she was done lying around. She needed answers, but in order to do that, she needed to get free. It was time to find out if she was alone or not. She yelled, "Jorge Salazar, I'm awake, so get your ass in here."

She waited one second, then another. Finally, the doorknob to her room turned and Jorge appeared in the doorway. "So, you're awake."

She narrowed her eyes. "Yes, I'm awake, asshole. And you'd better hope it's only the next morning, or I will find a way to hurt you later."

He merely raised an eyebrow. "Such big words from a lady currently tied to a bed. Have you ever considered being nice to me? That might work better at getting me on your side."

"Says the man who drugged me." She tugged on the restraints around her wrists. "Just answer me this: Is it only the next morning? And if so, what time is it?"

He gave a one-shoulder shrug. "It is. Why does the time matter?"

Okay, her headache was getting worse. "You know how I told you that I've been trying to bring the Fed League down since day one? Well, I have a contact that's been helping me and I need to meet him."

He moved toward her bed. "More secrets, Sabrina? What's his name? And how can this man help you? Answer those questions, and I'll consider letting you go so you can meet with him."

"Just like that?" She gave him a skeptical look. "That's way too easy. Now you're the one who is hiding something."

"I have a few other conditions, but just know that I have information on your waitress friend. That should encourage you to start talking."

"Okay, fine." *Think, Sabrina, think.* She'd have to tread carefully here. "His name is Juan Marquez. He has human friends with government connections. Watkins isn't only on your shit-list—he's wanted by the Mexican government."

"And how do you fit into all of this?"

"Well, I know Juan through Yolanda."

"The waitress? I watched you back in the restaurant before I approached you and you didn't seem like you were all that buddy-buddy."

"If there were even the slightest chance someone was watching you from the Fed League, would you want to act all buddy-buddy?"

"Good point." He took out a small pocketknife from one of the pockets of his pants and opened it. "So, let's say all of this is true. What are you supposed to meet and discuss with this Juan guy?"

She eyed the knife. She just needed to give him a little more information, and she might get free. "I'm close to getting Watkins, but I can't do it alone. I need backup, and that's where Juan comes in."

"Do you trust him?"

"With my life."

She swore she saw his jaw clench a second, but before she could blink, his face was relaxed again. He raised his knife and tapped the cloth restraints holding her arms with his blade as he said, "I can use all of the help I can get to capture Watkins, so I'll let you meet with this Juan guy, provided you agree to my conditions."

Great. Just what she needed. "They'd better not require me to be naked or for me to turn into your slave, because I can tell you right now that I'll refuse."

The corner of his lips twitched. "As much as I'd like you to be my naked sex slave, I was thinking more along the lines of you allowing me to shadow you to your meeting place to confirm your story. If it pans out, then your friend can help speed up our take-down of Watkins."

She knew she should stay focused, but she couldn't let Jorge's lip twitching pass. Before she could stop herself, Sabrina asked, "Wait a second—were you about to smile?"

~~*

Jorge had, indeed, nearly cracked a smile at Sabrina's flippant remark. Truth be told, he couldn't remember the last time he'd felt the urge.

But it was best to ignore her comment since he couldn't allow her to start liking him again. "Did you hear what I said? If you want free then you're going to have to let me follow you to the market. Afterward, once we regroup, you tell me what Juan says and I'll give you information on Yolanda."

Her teasing tone was gone. "Just tell me—is Yolanda in any immediate trouble?"

He suddenly felt guilty that he didn't have that much information to share with her. "If there were a way to save her right now, I swear to you that I would try to save her. But the information I have isn't enough for us to go looking for her. At least, not yet."

She looked at him for a few seconds and then sighed. "I'm probably an idiot for agreeing to this, but okay. Cut me free, and as long as you keep up your end of the bargain, I'll keep my promises."

He was probably no less an idiot, but the longer they kept butting heads and being stubborn, the greater the chance he would fail this mission. They needed to start working as a team, and this was as good a first step as any. "Fine," he said and then he took her wrist in his hand.

Her skin was much softer than his, and he couldn't help but brush his thumb against the warm underside of her wrist. Part of him wanted to keep her tied up so he could continue to look at her toned thighs, small but firm breasts, and the curve of her neck where it met her shoulder. He'd always been attracted to her, and it seemed that despite what needed to be done, and the fact she probably hated him more than ever before, he still was.

He gently slid his finger under the restraint and cut her free. Rather than give up her wrist, he massaged it with his fingers. He heard Sabrina's breath catch before she yanked her hand away. "We don't have time for you to play nice and care about my well-being. Just cut me free, let me use the restroom, and we can be on our way."

Her words snapped him back to reality. It was time to face facts—Sabrina would never want him, and fantasizing about her would only distract him from his mission.

Careful to touch her skin as little as possible this time, he cut her other wrist free and went down to her feet, making sure to face the bed and Sabrina. Good thing, too, since she sat up and started rotating her shoulders. With both of her legs free, he moved back and put away his knife. He motioned to the small en suite bathroom. "I'll give you ten minutes to clean up."

Since they both knew that there was no escaping through the tiny, barred window in the room, Sabrina nodded and he left to go check his phone one last time before they went to the market.

He didn't know whether it was a good or bad thing to not have any messages from his contacts, but he did notice the time. He only had twenty minutes before he could shift again. It was a good back-up plan to have if things went wrong during Sabrina's meeting with this Juan guy, but he hoped he didn't have to use it. He'd much rather use it later today to finish this damn mission so he could run as far away as possible from Sabrina and her warm, smooth skin.

~~*

Sabrina knew it was ridiculous, but she swore she could feel Jorge's eyes on her as she wandered the outdoor section of the market.

Ever since he'd caressed the underside of her wrist and massaged it, she'd become hyperaware of his presence. They had walked in near silence to this location, only speaking to lay out the basics of what would happen and their plans for any unexpected complications. But he'd bumped into her twice—once against her shoulder, and the other time against her hand—and both times she'd barely prevented herself from drawing in a breath. This part of Mexico was warm year-round, but her temperature had definitely knocked up a few degrees when his hand had brushed hers.

Her body had a hell of a way of noticing who was attractive. Considering he'd tied her up twice and drugged her, Jorge Salazar should be the last man she wanted. Well, except for maybe Watkins or any of his Fed League lackeys.

She swept the area with her eyes, determined to focus. She needed to find the clothing stand run by an elderly woman with her hair in a bun and dressed in a white Mayan-style loose top with blue and yellow embroidered flowers.

She and Juan rarely met in person, but each time it was at a different market and a different stall. The main thing was to pass on her information without looking suspicious. Someone else working for the *Feiru* Liaison office had previously confirmed that the elderly woman spoke no English—the language she and Juan usually used to communicate—so that wasn't the issue. No, the concern was always that someone might be watching either Juan or herself. Juan was retired from the field, but like any agent who'd spent years undercover on different assignments, he'd gained a few enemies over the years who'd like nothing more than to kill him.

It was a risk anyone from the office took when they agreed to go undercover.

She spotted the elderly woman she was looking for a few stands down, so Sabrina stopped at a spice stall in front of her and pretended to browse. She couldn't move to the clothing stall until she spotted Juan.

She made a token purchase of a small package of chili and moved to the next stall. That's when she noticed Juan, dressed in jeans and a blue polo shirt, walking down the main walkway toward her location. They briefly made eye contact, and then she moved to the clothing stall first.

SHADOW OF TEMPTATION

After holding up one of the Mayan-style embroidered blouses and asking about the price, Juan sidled up beside her. As he pretended to browse, she put down the shirt and picked up another. She held it high above her head to pretend to study the embroidery as she whispered, "There's been a change in plans. I have an additional helper for the final play, but I want some officials there to arrest our target."

"Who is this new helper?"

She shook her head. "No names. But he wants our target as much as we do."

Juan gave her a sideways glance. "You want me to risk my people on your word?"

She put down the shirt and picked up another one. "Yes. I may have to move up the date for my plan, but since my contact at the restaurant is missing, I'll need a new person to pass on the details."

Juan picked up one of the small purses embroidered with flowers and paid for it. He turned and managed to whisper, "We're looking for her. In the meantime, use the emergency phone number to contact me. If it's too dangerous to call me to get details, even in code, I'll find a way to give you the new contact's location. I'll start setting things up within the hour."

She nodded and Juan left. Sabrina put the shirt down, picked up the first one she had admired, and then paid the woman with a smile before she headed to one of the nearby stalls that sold shoes. She wanted to run straight to her meet-up location with Jorge, but she wasn't a rookie; she needed to keep shopping for at least another five or ten minutes to keep up appearances.

Still, things were looking good. While Yolanda might still be missing, Sabrina really had a shot at finishing this undercover stint in a day or two. She should feel happy at finally giving up this double-life of doing horrible things in order to help the greater good, but finishing the assignment meant that Jorge would leave and she'd never see him again.

She tried to convince herself that she didn't want him to leave until she could persuade him that she'd known nothing about him being passed on to the Collector. But deep down, she wanted more. She wanted the familiarity and ease they'd once had.

In short, she wanted to have a friend again.

And not just any friend—one who also made her skin heat with a touch and who could probably make her weak in the knees with a single kiss.

Ridiculous. Jorge would toss her to the wolves before he'd kiss her. Not that she could blame him. Her actions had killed his former feelings for her.

No, the best thing for her to do was to finish the job and send him on his way.

Sabrina moved to another stall and was about to buy some chopped fruit when she felt something slither around her bare ankle. She'd changed into the more civilian-looking clothes Jorge had provided before coming to the market—shorts, sandals, and a t-shirt—but when she glanced down, there was nothing. Yet it felt like a whisper of silk was brushing against her skin.

Careful to keep her face neutral, she tried to take a step, but something tugged at her ankle before changing directions. There was another tug, and Sabrina was forced to move her legs in the direction of the tugging or fall over. Another brush of silk on her other leg and she was soon being forced down the row of stands to the street. She tried not to look around, not wanting to draw attention to herself.

No, she only needed to get the attention of one person. She clenched her fingers into a fist and pointed her thumb downward—the signal that something was wrong.

She only hoped Jorge saw it.

Chapter Seven

While Jorge had been a prisoner under the Collector, his life had depended upon him learning to blend in, and today that skill was coming in handy at the crowded marketplace. His clothes were nondescript, and since he'd grown up near Merida during his childhood, even his accent wasn't noteworthy.

Still, it took some effort to keep an eye on Sabrina without deliberately staring at her. It had been a long time since he'd seen that much of her smooth, tan skin.

He'd been an idiot to choose jean shorts and a tight-fitting purple t-shirt from her apartment while she'd been unconscious. He should've gone with the jeans or one of her long flowing skirts. Then maybe he could concentrate on more than how the denim hugged her fine ass or how her shorts displayed almost every inch of her long, golden tan legs.

His thoughts had started to venture into more dangerous territory—such as how it'd feel to grab that soft, bare ass with his hands—when Sabrina finally approached the clothing stand she'd described as the meeting place.

This was it. Time to watch for this Juan guy and see what happened.

As she pretended to browse, a man with light brown skin and short black hair approached the same stall. Once Sabrina lifted up a shirt over her head as if to inspect it, he could see her lips moving. He didn't have supersensitive hearing or the ability to read lips, but from their interactions, he could tell they were at least somewhat familiar with each other. An average person wouldn't notice, but their mutual shared glances told him that they'd done this before.

He did a sweep of the surrounding market stalls to check for anything suspicious. He started to wonder just how well Sabrina knew this Juan guy when Jorge's eyes locked onto a face he'd seen once before. He didn't know the woman's name, but the long, red hair curling around her shoulders was unmistakable—the redhead was part of the Collector's army of *Feiru* with latent abilities.

Fuck. He wished he knew what sort of power she had, but he'd only glimpsed her once inside the Collector's facility. For good reason, the coerced soldiers hadn't been allowed to socialize.

He didn't want to break eye contact with the redhead, but he needed to check to see if Sabrina's meeting was over. Then he could start thinking of how to get her out of here, and preferably without the other woman following them.

He glanced back to the clothing stall and saw that Juan was already gone. Sabrina had just paid the woman running the stand when he noticed her foot move off to the side in an unnatural fashion.

He frowned when it happened again. Sabrina was hiding it well, but there was definitely something off about the way she walked—she lacked the slight sway of the hips and confidence to her strut. Instead, she was barely managing an uneven stroll. He glanced back to the redhead and saw her lips whispering something. He also noticed the motion of her thumb rubbing against her forefinger and middle finger. Those two actions told him what latent abilities the woman controlled.

The redhead was a Night-Weaver.

No matter how tight the Collector's security, people tended to talk with one another during missions. Most of his assignments had been solo kidnapping attempts, but during one multi-person kidnapping stint, he'd been forced to work with a man who'd been a Night-Weaver. He'd learned that they could weave strands as strong as steel yet they felt as soft as silk and the Night-Weaver could direct the strands to whatever target they chose. The bitch of it was that you could only see the strands at nighttime, when they'd glow a faint white from the moonlight. During the day, they were invisible to the naked eye.

If that weren't bad enough, there were probably other *Feiru* with latent abilities hiding in the market, waiting to take him down. If they managed to trap him and Sabrina in the midst of the crowded market, it could be game over. Even if he safely made it away from the prying eyes of humans, all the Collector's people needed to do was shoot him with some kind of tranquilizer and he wouldn't be able to use any of his shadow-shifting tricks to escape.

The Collector's soldiers had to be here, targeting Sabrina, because of him. He'd been careful, but someone had seen him, and he needed to do something. He wasn't about to let someone else be used against him again. Just the thought of Sabrina being tortured made him sick to his stomach. She might still be hiding some truths from him, but no one deserved the sort of abuse the Collector's people would inflict on her.

First things first, he needed to break the Night-Weaver's concentration long enough to get Sabrina to some of the nearby shadows. Once there, he could use one of his tricks to escape. But the question was: How?

He scanned the surroundings and saw a fruit stand off to his left. He quickly purchased a pineapple and moved closer toward Sabrina, careful to keep to the crowded edges of the vendor stands. By now, Sabrina was nearly to the street. If she reached it, a car could squeal up, snatch her, and take her anywhere. He needed to make his move before that could happen.

When Sabrina was less than five feet away from the sidewalk and the street, he lobbed the pineapple toward the Night-Weaver. A few people near him made some noise, but he ignored them. He watched closely because the second she stopped whispering and moving her fingers, he would make his move.

The Night-Weaver finally saw the incoming pineapple and stepped back right before it would've hit her.

With the redhead's concentration broken, Jorge grabbed Sabrina's upper arm and whispered, "We have to run. Come with me."

He didn't even wait for her to nod before he pulled her down one of the rows that split from the main walkway. He needed to reach the edge of the nearest building, preferably out of sight, where he could use the shadows to his advantage.

There was some shouting in the distance and Jorge knew the Collector's people had stopped trying to be inconspicuous. They had shifted into "capture at any costs" mode.

He shouldered his way through the throngs of people and made another turn, never easing his grip on Sabrina's arm. He could see a type of alley on the side of the building. At this time of day, it was all in shadow.

As soon as they reached the alley, Jorge shoved Sabrina up against the wall and caged her between his arms. "Whatever happens next, I need you to relax and not panic."

"Why? What's going on?"

"I'll explain later. For now, I'm about to show you one of my tricks and get us the hell out of here."

She glanced behind him and back. "Then hurry up. I can hear them coming."

He didn't have time to ponder the significance of her accepting his word so easily. Instead, he imagined the cells of his body breaking down, getting smaller and smaller. After two seconds, a familiar shock of pain flashed through his body and he became a dense shadow cloud.

Even though he no longer had eyes or ears, he was still aware of his surroundings. The Collector's soldiers were nearly upon them. He was going to have to pull his shadow-transport trick faster than he'd ever done before if they were to get away.

He still surrounded Sabrina in shadow form and he carefully covered her entire body with his shadowy mist. He started to caress her skin and she went limp. Any time he tried to transport someone, they always went unconscious; he didn't worry. Instead, he concentrated on engulfing her body. Once she was completely covered, he imagined her cells breaking down until she became part of his shadow cloud.

He could feel her warmth mixing with his own. In the past, he'd always had to transport strangers, and usually against their will. But this time was different. Sabrina was familiar, and her scent surrounded him and oddly calmed him. He was starting to realize how intimate this act was—two beings breaking down to become one.

Shit, that sounded way too romantic for his life, and he quickly pushed the thought aside.

Now that they were both shadows, he started to move along the darkest parts of the alley. He had done something similar a few days before, when he'd transported a man named Marco Alvarez from a different market.

Once they hit the streets, he easily avoided anyone stepping on or in him. The feeling of someone encroaching on his shadow form was never pleasant—like someone kicking him in the stomach or the side of the head.

Since he wasn't going to risk going back to the safe house in case their previous location had been compromised, Jorge headed to another place, one that would hopefully allow Sabrina enough time to wake up and recover. Now that the Collector's people had found them, the clock was ticking. They needed to move up their takedown of Watkins and flee the Yucatan peninsula as soon as possible if they wanted to live out the week.

~~*

Sabrina opened her eyes to find Jorge seated next to her on an unfamiliar bed and staring down at her. She tried to sit up, but he forced her to stay still with a hand on her shoulder. She glanced at his hand and back at his face before she asked, "Are you going to tell me what happened? One minute you disappear in front of my eyes, and the next I wake up here." She frowned. "Just what all can you do with those strange powers of yours?"

At first, she thought he was going to argue with her again, but instead, he studied her face. When he brushed a lock of hair off her forehead, she resisted a shiver at his touch—so tender and warm, a big contrast to his usual behavior.

That raised her guard. Why was he being so nice to her? The old Jorge might've been this tender, but not the newer, harder version. Something had to be wrong.

She glanced down, but she didn't see any life-threatening injuries. She looked back into his warm, brown gaze and said, "Do we really need to get into an arguing and threatening match again? Or will you just tell me what's going on?"

He stopped playing with her hair and said, "I didn't disappear back near the market. I used my shadow-shifting abilities to become a shadowy mist. That's what you saw all those months ago, when my arm seemingly 'disappeared' during our run. That had been the first time I'd ever had that happen to me."

She remembered that day. They'd been doing one of the trail runs on their day off. Jorge had suddenly buckled over and cried out in pain. She'd gone to him, convinced him to stand up, and then they'd both noticed the lack of his hand and forearm. Sabrina didn't remember screaming, but just staring with her mouth open. She'd heard a few tales of strange *Feiru* abilities during her early training with the *Feiru* Liaison office, but the disappearance of Jorge's arm had been the first time she'd seen any type of *Feiru* magic up close.

Once the shock had worn off, Jorge had pushed her aside and ran away. Sabrina had been too freaked out to follow him.

In hindsight, she realized how frightening the situation must have been for him. As his friend, she should've gone after him to make sure he was okay.

Instead, she'd betrayed him.

No. She wasn't going to walk down that memory lane again. Getting too close to him while undercover had been a huge mistake, and she couldn't let it happen again. Right now, she needed to focus on getting more information out of the man sitting beside her. Specifically, she needed to understand how his powers worked. Maybe then they could use them to help push up the date of their take down of Watkins.

SHADOW OF TEMPTATION

She needed to see Jorge Salazar as a tool and nothing more.

He was still staring at her with concern. She was pretty sure her face was neutral, but since her undercover agent training seemed to fade the longer she was around him, who the hell knew what the man saw.

Jorge raised his eyebrow in question, and she nodded for him to continue.

He rubbed the comforter on the bed between his fingers as he said, "What I did today was another aspect of my powers that I discovered during my time with the Collector. It's probably one of the few things I actually was happy to pick up."

"Is that how we got here?"

He nodded. "I can surround someone in my shadowy form and then break down their cells until they become a part of my shadow mist. As long as I don't shift back, I can move through the shadows and be nearly invisible. I call it my 'shadow-transport' ability, although I have no idea if that's what it's officially called or not."

She studied the young man in front of her. There was more that he wasn't telling her. "Not that I don't appreciate the explanations, but why are you suddenly telling me all of this without a fight? I could barely get two words out of you on the way to the market. What changed?"

His face turned grim. "Some of the Collector's army were back at the market. That's why you had trouble walking, because someone with the ability to weave strong, invisible strands and direct them to move as they wished had control over your legs. The female Night-Weaver—that's the name of that latent ability—was there because of me. If you'd been taken, they would've done the same to you as my sister, maybe even worse. And no one, not even you, deserves that."

She softened a little at his words. Maybe he didn't hate her as much as she'd thought. "Why would they go after me? It's not like I mean anything to you."

His jaw clenched. "They probably saw me carrying you from your apartment to that other safe house. They had no way of knowing that you were merely drugged and not curled up against my chest."

All of the tender thoughts she had about him vanished. "Next time, you should just put up a huge sign. That way they won't make the same mistake twice." She tried to sit up, but he kept her in place with his hand on her shoulder. "Let me up, Jorge. The sooner we figure out our next steps, the sooner you can leave and never see me again."

Anger flashed in his eyes. "Two things. One, you need to rest a little longer to recuperate from becoming part of my shadow mist or you'll end up fainting." He lowered his head until he was a few inches from her face. "And two, it matters to me if you live or die, so stop dismissing yourself as expendable, because you're not."

His breath was hot against her cheek, and she couldn't look away from his gaze. "What?"

"Knowing the Collector's people like I do, it won't be long before they find me. If I'm going to die soon, then I'm going to stop pretending around you." He moved so that he caged her body with his arms. "For whatever fucked up reason, I still want you, maybe even more than I did as the nice guy from all those months ago. But what I need to know, Sabrina, is if your indifference is the same or if you've changed your mind?" He lifted a hand to run a finger down her cheek and her breath hitched. His eyes turned heated. "Just say the word, Sabrina, and

I'll kiss you." He leaned close until he was a hairbreadth away from her lips. "Maybe even more. So tell me, what should I do?"

Her heart was pounding so loud that she wondered if Jorge could hear it. He continued to stroke her cheek, and each pass of his finger was like a little shock that went straight to her core. In that second, she wanted him naked and inside her.

The realization should startle her, but Sabrina was tired of lying to herself. She wanted him to kiss her more than anything she'd wanted in a long time. But she hadn't survived this long by simply seizing what she wanted. She needed to make sure that indulging in a kiss wouldn't screw up their plans or endanger their safety.

If she could secure that, then maybe—just maybe—she could finally do something because she wanted to do it instead of doing it for the sake of the mission. "Won't the Collector's people be looking for us? We should probably think of where to hide and see if it's still possible to stop Watkins's plan."

He moved his finger from her cheek to her lower lip, his finger warm and rough against her sensitive skin. It took everything she had not to moan.

Jorge stilled his finger and said, "There is no way they could've followed my shadow escape. We need to lay low for at least a few hours before we do anything." He moved his finger from her lip to under her chin and lifted. "Stop thinking of excuses. We're safe for now, so if you want me, then say it. Life's too short to keep denying what you truly want."

His proximity, his touch, his heat, and his masculine scent filling her nose were all too much. She couldn't—and didn't want to—resist him any longer.

Sabrina ran a hand up to his neck, pulled down until he rested his body against hers, and whispered, "Kiss me."

Chapter Eight

Jorge could barely believe his ears. He hadn't expected Sabrina to say yes, let alone pull him down against her body and look at him as if she was ready to devour him. Before she could change her mind, he cupped the side of her face and lowered his lips to hers.

He kissed her gently at first, but the first taste of her lips sent blood straight to his cock, and he desperately wanted to see if the combination of her taste in his mouth and her scent in his nose would be as addictive as he imagined.

He may have tried to deny it, but he'd wanted this woman for nearly two years. He pushed aside any hesitation and brushed the seam of her lips for permission. She opened and he plunged into her sweet, warm mouth. The heady combination of her heat and taste made him moan. He wanted more, much more.

But was he the only one? He decided to find out.

He moved his hand to the hem of Sabrina's t-shirt and ran his finger under the material to brush the soft, smooth skin of her waist with his fingers. The more he stroked, the more Sabrina moaned into his mouth, and he knew she wanted more, too.

He eased off her chest and slowly ran his hand under her shirt until he could cup her breast over her bra. He could feel her tight, beaded nipple through the material and he took a chance and pinched the tight bud. Sabrina threaded her fingers through his hair and stroked her tongue more fervently against his own.

Wanting to see if he could make her even crazier with desire, he pinched and rolled her nipple again as he fought for control of her mouth, reveling in their teeth clashing more than once as they each fought for control. Sabrina met him stroke for stroke and upped her game by wrapping one of her legs around his and raising her hips against his cock. Despite the clothes separating their skin, he thrust against her and Sabrina broke the kiss with a hiss.

He stilled his lower body and whispered, "Look at me."

Her heated brown gaze met his, and his cock throbbed, demanding much more than the friction of clothing against clothing. He wanted her skin.

He pulled down one of the cups of Sabrina's bra under her shirt and rubbed his palm against her hard, beaded nipple. "Will you let me taste you, Sabrina?"

He pinched her nipple and she moved her hips against him as she whispered, "Yes."

After giving her breast one last squeeze, he moved his hand to the bottom of her shirt and tugged up. She raised her arms; he lifted the shirt off, and tossed it aside. He looked down and the image of one smooth, tan breast exposed while the other was still covered with her blue bra made him even harder.

Sabrina lifted her hand to his hair again and pulled down. "Are you going to keep staring or are you going to taste me, like you promised?"

Fuck, he didn't know what he'd done to deserve this sexy, straightforward woman, but he was going to relish every minute of it while it lasted.

He growled, bent down, and sucked her nipple. Hard. He felt her other leg wrap around his waist, but he focused on teasing her tight bud with his tongue. A swirl, a flick, and then he finally bit her gently. She tightened her grip in his hair and he released her. He blew on her wet flesh and she shivered. He smiled. "Maybe I should stop there."

"The hell you will." Sabrina grabbed his head and brought it down to her face.

~~*

Sabrina didn't know what had come over her, but all she knew was that from the instant Jorge had kissed her, all of her years of pent-up lust had come rushing forth.

At least that was what her mind wanted to rationalize, but Sabrina had never wanted a man to fuck her as much as she wanted the man currently between her legs. His warmth, his strength, and even his taste made every inch of skin sensitive and aware that she was a woman and he was a man.

The way he tortured her nipple had nearly made her come. When he blew on her wet skin and suggested he should stop, she was beyond the point of rational thought. So, she took what she wanted, grabbed his head, and kissed him.

She pushed her tongue inside his mouth and arched her back up to rub her sensitive nipples against his chest. The friction of one bared breast and one bra-covered against the fabric of his shirt was a different kind of sensation than what she'd had before, but it wasn't enough. She wanted to feel the heat of his skin around, over, and inside her.

Jorge had taken control of her mouth again, making her breathless with his strokes and nips, but somehow she managed to break the kiss. Between pants, she managed to whisper, "Take off your shirt."

Shadow of Temptation

She barely had a chance to blink before his shirt was tossed to the floor. She raised a hand to his chest and ran her fingers over his smooth, hard muscles. He grabbed her hand. She looked up and her heart skipped a beat. She saw something she hadn't seen since his return to Merida—mischief in his eyes and a playful smile on his face. Just as she'd thought, he wasn't a total lost cause.

He squeezed her hand against his chest and his voice was husky when he said, "I've shown you mine, now show me yours."

He stared down at her still covered breast, released her hand, and tugged her bra down. He flicked her nipple before he ran his hands over her breasts and around her sides. "Arch up for me, baby."

She did, and he unhooked her bra with slow, deliberate movements. Each brush of his warm fingers on her skin sent wetness between her thighs.

But she was impatient. Due to the nature of her work, it'd been years since she'd had sex, and Sabrina was done with waiting.

She was about to push his hands aside and unhook her bra herself when he finally yanked her bra free and tossed it aside. She reached for him again, but Jorge shook his head and stared at her bared breasts. She'd never been shy about her body, but right now, with his hot gaze on her skin, she flushed.

His eyes took a devilish glint and he cupped the side of her breasts with his hands as he started to rub his thumb across her nipples. Each rough pass against her throbbing skin made her wetter. She whispered, "Jorge, please."

He released her right breast and traced a finger down her ribcage to the waistband of her shorts. "I want to rip these off and fuck you, but I don't have any protection. Do you?"

Shit. She shook her head. "No, I haven't needed to worry about that for a long time." He smiled at her remark and she narrowed her eyes. "Why are you smiling? I want to be naked and sweaty from sex, and now that's not going to happen. With who knows how many people on the lookout for you, it's not like you can run to the drugstore."

He unbuttoned her shorts and slowly unzipped them. "I'm smiling because I've fantasized a long time about making you come with my tongue."

Suddenly all she could think about was Jorge's head between her thighs, licking and suckling her to orgasm. "Oh."

He grinned and she stopped breathing for a second. She reached up and laid a hand on his arm. She wanted to tell him how good it was to see him smile, but she was afraid that mentioning it would bring his past back into the bed and kill the mood. Instead, she said, "Stop teasing me and prove you can do it."

His grin faded into something much hotter. "For that, I'm going to take my time and lick oh so slowly until you're so frustrated you'll be begging me to finish."

His words sent a rush of wetness straight between her legs, and her clit was pulsing in anticipation. But she wasn't going to surrender that easily. She opened her mouth to reply when someone knocked on the door.

What the hell? Had someone actually found them?

Sabrina's training kicked into action the same time as Jorge's. She sat up as he moved to the side of the bed and took out two guns from the nightstand. He placed one on the bed next to her and his voice was low when he said, "Put your shirt on and cover me."

Sabrina nodded and grabbed her shirt from the floor. Jorge went to the door as she tossed the shirt over her head. She picked up the gun, clicked off the safety, and took position to where she had a clear line of sight to the door but could still dive for cover if she needed it.

She nodded and Jorge turned the lock. She could see the chain still latched across the door, which would give them a few extra seconds to react if things went south.

He placed his hand on the doorknob and slowly twisted it open. He gave her one more look before he inched the door open. Before he could say anything, a woman with accented English said, "Jorge Salazar, it's bad form to keep a lady waiting on the doorstep. Now, my dear, open this door and invite me in. Despite your ungrateful behavior—of course who could blame you? I'd be cross too if someone interrupted my sexy times—I still might share my bag of pastries with you and Sabrina."

Sabrina blinked. She wondered who the hell was the woman on the other side of the door and how she knew her name.

~~*

Jorge had no idea who the woman on the other side of the door was, but her words about "sexy times" made him think that, despite all of his precautions, someone had stashed a camera somewhere in the room. The idea of someone else seeing Sabrina's naked breasts didn't sit well with him.

Right now, however, he needed to try to think of the best way to play this since he couldn't use his shadow-shifting abilities again until tomorrow.

Asking the woman for her identity would be useless. They might have to use the hidden escape door behind the wardrobe—

that had been the entire reason he'd chosen this location out of his handful of places to lay low. Even when he'd worked for the Fed League, he had wanted backup escape routes in case something went wrong.

He caught Sabrina's eye and put up a hand with all five fingers. He nodded his head to the wardrobe and back. Sabrina understood that he had a plan—even if she didn't know what it was—and nodded back. He lowered one finger and then another before the woman on the other side of the door spoke again. "If you try to escape through the secret passage behind the wardrobe, I most definitely will not share my pastries with you."

He stopped the countdown. Even if there was a camera in the room, and the woman outside had seen him nod toward the wardrobe, no one knew about his secret passageway. With that comment, he couldn't stop himself from asking, "Who are you?"

"I'm surprised Aislinn didn't mention me. Hmph. I'll have to talk to her about that." The woman waved a few fingers through the door. "Hello, my name is Neena Chatterjee. I help run DEFEND, and I highly advise you to let me inside unless you want me to start drawing attention from people down on the street."

Aislinn was the woman who had organized the rescue for his sister last week. Still, this Neena hadn't given him specific enough information for him to believe her yet. He needed to know more. "Prove that you work with Aislinn—tell me where they found my sister."

Neena removed her fingers and her voice was serious when she answered, "Tied-up naked in a freezer, on a sprawling estate about an hour from Merida, off the main road to Celestún."

Her answer was correct. He still wanted to question her further, but he wanted to do it away from possible prying eyes.

"Okay, I'll open the door, but I want you to have your hands raised when I let you in to make sure you don't have any weapons."

Neena answered, "I don't usually take orders, but just this once, I'll agree."

Before the woman started talking again, he unchained the door and slowly opened it until he had a short woman with wild, curly black hair and golden tan skin standing in front of him. Her hands were up, and she had a clear plastic bag of Mexican pastries in her left hand.

He only hoped the pastries didn't hide something much worse inside of them.

He waved her inside. "Hurry up."

She walked in, and since he knew Sabrina would watch his back, he locked the door before turning around to find Neena giving Sabrina the once-over.

Despite the fact Sabrina had to be as confused as hell as to what was going on, she was alert and had her gun trained on Neena. Sabrina's trust in him chipped away even more at his belief she'd turned him in on purpose. But if he were ever to have a discussion with Sabrina and possibly get her naked again, he needed to make sure they survived this encounter.

He gave Neena a wide berth and stopped a few feet away from both Neena and Sabrina. Before he could ask Neena a question, the woman tilted her head and said, "The sooner you lower your guns and talk with me, the sooner you can plan your take-down of Watkins. Once that's done, I'll let you have a week off to hump each other like rabbits. Or whatever animal mating rituals you fancy imitating. Horses, perhaps? Or turtles? No one ever says, 'hump like turtles'."

Jorge ignored her needling. "How about you start talking some sense? After this job, you have no say in what I do."

Neena shook her head. "Tsk, tsk. Sometimes I forget not everyone knows what's going to happen." She looked at Sabrina. "Like Sabrina here. She has a very big secret, one that should lead to a wonderful partnership in the future. DEFEND could use the help of her employer."

He wasn't going to completely just take this Neena at her word, especially since he didn't know if Sabrina had an actual employer outside the Fed League or not. "Why would your precious organization need her help? Once the Fed League crumbles, she'll move on to something else."

Neena glanced to him. "Why don't you ask her? I'm sure she's heard of DEFEND and could see why her employer might be of some value to me and my organization."

He growled at Neena. "Sabrina, tell her you aren't working for anyone else so I can tell this woman she's crazy."

Sabrina remained silent, so he darted a glance to her face and back to Neena. Even in that split second, he could see how pale she'd become. "Sabrina?"

Neena smiled. Her voice was calm and coaxing when she said, "Go on, my dear, tell him. I promise you won't be 'relocated' and banished for the rest of your life. You have no reason to trust me, but surely you've heard about the 'colorful' DEFEND co-leader and her reach. That's me, and if you cooperate, I'll protect you."

Jorge looked to Sabrina again. "I'm lost. What's she talking about? Who do you work for?"

CHAPTER NINE

Sabrina stared at the woman who called herself Neena Chatterjee. Somewhere in Sabrina's basic training, she'd heard of the eccentric DEFEND leader and her knack for always showing up at a critical time to sway things her way. Sabrina had dismissed most of the rumors as bullshit, but she was starting to reconsider her call.

Then Neena had to mention how Sabrina had a secret to share, and she barely resisted panicking.

So many things had happened in the last few hours with Jorge. She had started to think she'd tell him the full truth, but this was not the way she'd imagined it—half-rumpled and bra-less, pointing a gun at a strange woman clinging to a bag of pastries.

The strange woman in question had assured her she wouldn't be relocated if worse came to worse, but she didn't trust her word. Instead, she cleared her throat and chanced a quick glance at Jorge. "Before I say anything, I want to know why you give any credence to her words. Why does mentioning this Aislinn person mean anything to you?"

He looked like he wanted to press her to answer, but after he gave a glance to Neena, he looked back at her and said, "Aislinn is the one who orchestrated my sister's rescue. There is more to the story than that, but if you have any faith in me at all, then let that be enough for now." He waved his free hand toward

Neena. "Please answer her question. The sooner you do, the sooner she'll leave."

"Hmph," Neena said but kept her attention on Sabrina. "Maybe I can help ease your worry. That'll make this easier for all of us."

Before Sabrina could open her mouth, she felt a gentle breeze brush against her skin. Normally, she'd jump away and try to figure out what was going on, but a sense of calm and trust came over her like she could tell Neena anything, without fear.

She shook her head to try to break the feeling, but the sense of calmness only increased to the point where Sabrina was as languid as if she'd had three orgasms and an hour-long hot bath. She frowned and said, "What did you do to me?"

Neena smiled. "Don't worry, my dears, it'll wear off soon. But I'm on a tight schedule and this is the easiest way to speed things along. You'll both thank me later." She lowered her hands and took out a pastry. "Now, tell us about your employer."

Sabrina didn't feel compelled to say anything, but the false sense of trust loosened her usual secretive nature and the truth just spilled out. "I'm working undercover for the *Feiru* Liaison office in Mexico City."

From the corner of her eye, she saw Jorge shake his head, as if to knock away whatever Neena Chatterjee had done to them. "But that means..."

His voice trailed off, and Sabrina decided to bite the bullet and tell him the truth. "I'm human."

~~*

Jorge wasn't sure how to reply to Sabrina's confession. He felt a little betrayed and somewhat concerned, but he could barely frown because of what Neena Chatterjee had done to him. Standing up was a chore. Arguing would take too much energy.

But if nothing else, he could make his voice work and ask questions. He needed to hear a hell of lot more from Sabrina to believe what she'd just told him. "You've been human this whole time? How is that possible? The Fed League does blood tests to ensure everyone who joins is at least half-*Feiru*."

Sabrina squared her shoulders. Considering she was a weak human in a room with a Shadow-Shifter and a who-the-hell-knew-what crazy magic user, she was brave. He nearly whispered, "Good girl," but then he remembered what she'd just said and waited for her to explain.

He didn't have to wait long.

"I'm not about to spill all of the *Feiru* Liaison office's secrets, but we've found a way around the blood tests. I underwent the necessary treatment, and I passed without a hitch."

His first objection answered, Jorge realized the enormity of her confession. He managed to take a step toward her, but he faltered and barely managed to keep from falling over. "You were already in the Fed League when I joined. Just how long have you been undercover? Has everything been a lie?"

"It's been about two years. But no, not everything has been a lie." She darted a glance to Neena—who was chomping on a pastry of all things—and then back to him. Her voice was low when she said, "I hate causing people harm, let alone like participating in assignments that result in deaths. But your friendship was the one thing I never regretted. You helped to keep me sane, Jorge Salazar, and I hope you won't hate me for keeping this from you."

He hadn't expected that confession.

He ran a hand through his hair and said, "I can't deal with all of this right now." He pointed a finger at Neena. "Stop eating that damn pastry and tell me why you're doing all of this. You seem to have more information than me or Sabrina about Watkins, the Fed League, and even the *Feiru* Liaison officers. So why the hell aren't you doing all of this yourself? Is this just a game to you? Because let me tell you, this is our fucking lives, and I, for one, don't like people playing with them."

Neena chewed the last bit of pastry in her mouth and brushed the crumbs from her hands. "I know you had a rough time of it with the Collector, but you're going to have to work on those manners of yours. You can be alpha and pushy all you like with anyone else, but you'll soon learn that I won't tolerate it."

He growled. "Manners? What the hell do they matter? Being nice is what ended up getting me fucked up in the first place."

Neena sniffed and looked toward Sabrina. "I'm not sure how you straight women deal with men. Frankly, they're too much work."

Sabrina's mouth dropped, but Jorge didn't care about whether Neena preferred men or women. He was tired of the lies and answer dodging.

He stumbled over to Neena and grabbed her arm. Before he knew what was going on, he felt a prick in his side and the room started to spin. "What the hell?"

He fell to his knees and then tumbled to the carpet. Neena's voice was faint when she replied. "You're going to take a little nap while I talk with Sabrina here. I'm sure she can have a rational conversation without needing to bang her fists against her chest like a caveman."

Sabrina's face came into view. "Jorge?" She put a hand on his cheek and her touch helped to ease his anger. "What did you do to him?"

"Don't worry, he'll be fine. The nap will actually do him some good."

He tried to reach a hand to touch Sabrina's thigh next to him, but he lacked the strength to move. The last thought he had before he blacked out was that Sabrina was going to be left alone with the crazy woman, and he wouldn't be able to protect her.

~~*

Sabrina caressed Jorge's cheek, but he didn't respond. He was out cold.

Anger welled up inside her at what Neena had done to Jorge. She'd been too sluggish to stop Neena from injecting him with some type of drug, and now he lay on the floor, helpless. She'd just have to protect him until he woke up. He might be angry at her for keeping secrets, but the look he'd given her right before he'd passed out told her volumes about how much he didn't hate her.

Despite learning she was human, he still might even want her.

However, she'd never get the chance to talk with him about it if they both ended up dead.

She tried to think of how she could trick the woman behind her. Because of her fear for Jorge's safety or her anger for Neena attacking him, Sabrina had no idea, but whatever Neena had done to her earlier was starting to wear off. The best she could do was pretend to still be under the effects of the woman's magic and find a way to restrain her.

She still had the gun gripped in her right hand. If she could just knock the woman unconscious, she could tie her up and get answers that way.

Sabrina shifted her feet and was about to try out her plan when she heard Neena's voice. "Despite his obvious lack of manners, you feel something for that man and you want to protect him, but fighting me isn't the way to do it. If you listen long enough, I can give you the information you need to take down Watkins tonight."

Sabrina nearly fell for it, but she wasn't going to let the woman sweet-talk her into anything. She rose slowly and faced Neena, keeping her body ready to pounce at a moment's notice. "If you think I'm going to trust you, you're crazy. Jorge did, and look what happened to him."

"I helped him. The drug I injected will help his body regain the necessary energy to shift again. He won't have to wait until tomorrow. By the time he wakes up, he'll be ready to go." Neena tilted her head. "You can apologize any time you like, my dear. The sooner you stop planning to attack me, the sooner I can give you the information you need and get out of your hair. Believe me, I have a million other things I'd rather be doing right now than trying to convince people not to kill me. Besides, I'm your best bet at avoiding relocation and isolation for the rest of your life."

As if she'd take that bait. She didn't trust Neena, but she did have an idea. "How about you tell me the information you have on Watkins and leave? Do it without a fight, and I might consider trusting and using the information you provide."

Neena shrugged. "If that's how you want to play it. Just put the safety back on your gun, and I'll spill the beans."

Since she could still use the gun to whack Neena upside the head if something happened, she did as she was asked. "Now, tell me what you know."

Neena moved to the window and sat down on the sill. "Let's not forget our manners. Say please."

Sabrina grit her teeth. At this point, she'd do anything to get this woman to leave. "Fine. Please tell me what you know."

"Better. I'm starting to see why you and Mr. Grouchy-pants over there get along so well."

She took a deep breath and decided it was best to ignore the comment and press Neena for answers. "I said please; now tell me how I can get Watkins tonight."

Neena sniffed. "Fine. He's going to move up the school bombing. He'll be installing the device himself this evening."

"What? Why?"

Neena waved a hand. "Some rival nonsense, blah, blah, blah. Basically, Watkins is afraid you'll share his plans and he'll have to abort his mission, and this is one he can't afford to screw up."

She studied Neena a moment and finally said, "And how do I know you're telling the truth? Sure, you claim that drugging Jorge will help him, but I have no idea if that's even possible. The holes in the *Feiru* Liaison office's knowledge about the *Feiru* and their abilities are big enough to drive a train through."

Neena crossed one leg over another. "I'll tell you something that might convince you, but I'd suggest that you take a seat first."

"I prefer to stand."

Neena shrugged. "Fine, although you might change your mind. You see, I have some bad news for you, my dear. Do you know how that Night-Weaver found you at the market?"

Sabrina frowned. How did Neena know about that? "Jorge said it was because someone saw him with me, and that the Collector woman planned to use me to coerce him again."

Neena made a buzzing sound with her voice. "Wrong. They were there because Watkins tortured Yolanda until she told them about you and your relationship with the *Feiru* Liaison office. By decoding your message, he knew about your meeting with Juan Marquez and sent the Night-Weaver and others to capture you."

Sabrina's heart skipped a beat. Juan's name wasn't common knowledge. "My identity is compromised?" Neena nodded and she forced herself to ask, "What about Yolanda?"

Neena shook her head. "I'm sorry, but she didn't make it, my dear."

Somehow Sabrina managed to keep on her feet. Now was not the time to grieve for the woman she'd barely known, but who had continuously risked her life to help Sabrina's mission. The best thing she could do was finish this damn assignment and make sure Watkins was put into custody to receive justice.

She took a step toward Neena. "I've been working for the *Feiru* Liaison office for a little over five years, and your knowing all of this is too much of a coincidence. Tell me how you got this information and I might start to believe we're on the same side."

"Clever girl." Neena buffed the nails of her right hand against her shirt and looked at them. "First, answer me this: What does your office know about latent abilities?"

"Only rumors, and most of them are from nearly a hundred years ago. Why?"

Neena looked up. "While Salazar's ability is pretty nifty, I have the rarest ability of them all. In addition to being an elemental wind first-born, I can see snippets of the future."

"What?"

"You say that a lot for no reason." Neena uncrossed her leg and stood up. "I told you, I can see bits of the future. While things can always change, I have a pretty good track record of figuring out what will come true or not. And for you, my dear, I think I'll be right again."

Sabrina avoided saying "what" again. Her mind was clear enough to fall back on her years of intelligence gathering. In any situation, it came down to asking the right question at the right time.

She was pretty confident that Neena wouldn't divulge Sabrina's own future, but there was something she wanted to know, something that would affect the whole world. "Okay, so tell me what's going to happen to *Feiru* and human relations in the future?"

Neena's face grew serious. "A lot of people will die, but eventually the *Feiru* will live side-by-side with the humans and the way we both live will change forever."

She studied Neena's features and body language, but if she were lying, she was damn good. Besides, Sabrina's gut told her Neena believed her words to be true. She didn't look forward to the "a lot of people will die" part of the prediction, but she only hoped the integration of the races would lead to a better tomorrow worth the sacrifice.

"Fine. I'll talk with Jorge about going after Watkins tonight. For now, I think it's time for you to leave."

Neena smiled. "I have an ever-growing list of things to do, so I think I will leave. But I'll see you again soon."

Jorge moved on the ground and Sabrina looked at him a second before she glanced back to where Neena had been standing. The woman was gone.

She brushed off her irritation. The woman was annoying, but if she were right, tonight would be big. If Jorge could confirm that his powers were recharged and ready to use, she would finally finish this assignment. That thought sent a thrill through her—one mixed with relief and a little bit of fear. Now that her identity had been compromised, either she would spend the rest of her life at a desk job in some secret location, or the *Feiru* Liaison office would "relocate" her to who the hell knew where.

But at the moment, none of that mattered. She moved to Jorge's location on the floor and sat beside him. He was restless and moving about as if he were having an active dream. She put a hand on his forehead and he calmed.

She stroked his hair and hoped he woke up soon. She wanted to finish this business with Watkins so she could talk to him about her revelation. She had no idea what he would think of her being human.

Part of her hoped he would accept her, but another part of her was afraid that this would be one lie too many and he'd never learn to trust her ever again.

CHAPTER TEN

Harry Watkins watched the woman with dark skin and short, curly black hair sitting in the chair in front of him. She was silent with her eyes closed, gripping the pillowcase his people had retrieved from Ono's apartment. It wasn't in his nature to be patient, but this woman was extremely valuable to the Collector. If he harmed her in any way, Watkins wouldn't live to see tomorrow.

There were few people who could threaten him and mean it. The Collector was one of them.

So he waited with his arms crossed over his chest. The woman in the chair was a Locator. All she needed was something that had been worn or touched by a person in the last twenty-four hours, and she could pinpoint their approximate location down to twenty or thirty feet. It wasn't an exact science, but Watkins would use whatever he could to find the traitor.

Earlier, his men had succeeded in breaking the waitress, and she'd told them as much as she knew about Sabrina Ono. The only important facts had been that Ono worked for the *Feiru* Liaison office, she'd had a meeting with her office's boss this morning, and she was human.

His borrowed latent soldiers had fucked up this morning, which had led to him using the Locator's abilities. Watkins needed to find Ono. She was the only real threat capable of ruining his plan against his rival, which he needed to succeed to please the

Collector. Since Ono was determined to thwart his plans, he needed to find her before she could finish the job. The tricky part was the Shadow-Shifter, Jorge Salazar, seemed to be working with her. *Feiru* with latent abilities were always harder to catch, but since Salazar had used his shadow-shifting abilities to escape earlier today, he'd be easy to capture until tomorrow, when the man could shift again.

The woman in the chair gasped and opened her eyes. She blinked a few times and then looked Watkins in the eye. "I think I've pinpointed her location."

"Where?"

"Not far from the zoo. I can see the row of small rectangular houses, but I won't be able to pinpoint exactly which one until I see it."

He nodded. "Right. Take my team of men and women, as well as the Siren. Use her if you need to, but just bring me Sabrina Ono. Salazar is secondary, but both I and the Collector would reward you if you could bring him in as well."

The woman's face was blank as she nodded, which was the normal expression for any of the Collector's long-term soldiers. Watkins signaled to his men in the room to assist the Locator out. Once she was gone, he brought up the video conference program on his computer and waited for the Collector to answer. As always, her face was shielded from view, but her voice was clear when she asked, "Did you find the woman?"

"Yes. Your Locator is on her trail, and no doubt Salazar is with her. Did you need both of them alive?"

"For now. The Shadow-Shifter has his uses, but it's the woman I want. Rumors have been floating around the *Feiru* Liaison offices about a tip from James Sinclair, and this woman might give me the edge I need to keep Sinclair otherwise occupied."

Watkins didn't know—nor care—about the Collector's other plans, but in the interest of keeping civil, he nodded. "I'll pass on the message. I wanted to ask for some reinforcements so I can focus on the bombing whilst your people take care of Ono and Salazar."

"They're already on their way. Contact me when everything is complete."

The screen went blank and Watkins picked up his cell phone to call his bomb makers. He just might be able to pull this all off before breakfast tomorrow.

~~*

Jorge waited behind the large wooden desk in his shadow form. Any minute now, his target would enter and he'd have only seconds to engulf the man, knock him unconscious, and absorb him into his mist.

The target was a local police detective sympathetic to the Feiru, *a man named Julio Reyes. Jorge wasn't supposed to know why Reyes was the target, but while sniffing around and determining the best way to kidnap the man, he'd learned of Reyes's current investigation into some* Feiru-related crimes.

He didn't know all the particulars, but some of the crimes were by prominent gangs in the area, gangs that had been previous targets of the Collector. Jorge's best guess was that the Collector didn't want any of the human authorities putting their noses into her business.

He almost felt bad for the human, but if Jorge failed this assignment, he knew his sister would be tortured again. No matter what it took, he couldn't allow that to happen.

The lock turned and Jorge watched the door, but instead of Reyes, he saw Harry Watkins holding a knife to his sister Alejandra's throat. He moved toward Watkins, but the man slit Alejandra's throat before he could reach the pair. Jorge watched in horror as his sister's lifeless body was tossed to the floor. Watkins kicked her and stared straight at him. "You're no different than me. You've killed innocents, and so have I. Remember that."

Watkins vanished and Jorge watched his sister's blood cover the floor, unable even to cry out at his sister's murder.

Jorge jerked awake and sat up, heaving in deep breaths. Something touched his back and he rolled off the bed to the side and took a defensive crouch. He looked up to see Sabrina staring at him with a mixed expression of puzzlement and concern.

Her voice was soft when she asked, "Are you okay?"

He drew in a deep sigh. He'd been dreaming. Alejandra was safe with DEFEND, not dead on the floor.

When he still didn't answer, Sabrina moved to where he was crouched and kneeled on the floor in front of him. She reached a hand toward him and he suddenly yearned for her comforting touch, but then she pulled back and he wondered why. She asked, "How do you feel? Were you just having a bad dream or a negative reaction to Neena's drugs?"

Neena. The crazy woman's name brought him back to the present and what had happened. He did another quick scan of the room, but he didn't see Neena anywhere. "I'm fine. It was just a bad dream, don't worry about it. What happened to Neena? Tell me what happened after that woman drugged me."

She raised an eyebrow. "You don't look fine to me."

"Sabrina."

She put up her hands. "Fine, I'll drop it for now. As for what happened, you're probably not going to like it."

Now that his heart rate had calmed a little, his head ached. He slowly stood up and realized the sluggishness from earlier was gone. "Tell me anyway. It'll give me a chance to try to pull myself together and shake off any aftereffects of the drugs Neena pumped into me."

She also stood up and watched him for a second before she finally replied. "Well, Neena and I had a chat."

"A chat? Seriously? With the crazy lady who drugged me unconscious?"

She shrugged. "Hey, I was ready to knock her out cold until she said some things that forced me to take her seriously. Did you know she can see visions of the future? The woman has abilities I can't even name."

He took a step toward Sabrina. "I may have heard something about that, but enough about Neena's abilities. Just tell me what she said."

She crossed her arms over her chest. "She gave me the information we needed to take down Watkins tonight."

"Exactly how is this supposed to happen? I can't even shift until tomorrow morning."

She shook her head. "You're wrong. I don't know how your abilities work, but if you can 'check' on your power levels, they should be at full capacity thanks to a mystery drug."

He gave her a skeptical look. "I've never heard of a drug like that. If it existed, I'm sure the Collector would've used it."

"Just check, okay? For me? If what Neena told me about this drug recharging your powers is true, then I'd feel more confident about using the other information she gave me."

He stared and she stared back. He could tell the woman wasn't going to back down.

The human had guts; he'd give her that. *Human.* He'd nearly forgotten about her earlier revelation, but for some reason it didn't seem to bother him as much as he'd expected. Probably because of the way she'd looked at him when he'd fallen to the ground earlier. It'd been a long time since someone had shown any concern or worry for him.

He just needed to be careful not to read too much into it.

He sighed. "Fine. I can't believe I'm doing this, but I have a feeling you'll argue with me until I do what you ask, so in the interest of saving time, give me a second." He closed his eyes and focused on the hum of power he drew on whenever he used his shadow-shifting abilities. Normally, this close after using them, it would be nothing more than a whisper. But Sabrina was right—his energy was pulsing at full power.

He opened his eyes. "Usually shifting so close together would put enough strain on my heart to kill me, but my energy levels are back to full. I can shift again without killing myself. How is that possible?"

"The drug I mentioned was the one Neena injected you with, and it seems she was telling the truth about it speeding up your recovery process."

He opened his mouth to ask how, but decided that wasn't important right now. Instead, he said, "But there must be more you aren't telling me because as awesome as I am with my abilities, they alone won't capture Watkins."

~~*

Sabrina couldn't get the look of horror she'd seen on Jorge's face when he'd jumped up from his bad dream out of her head. She wanted to wrap him in a hug and push him to tell her

94

what it'd been about, but she had a feeling he wouldn't say a word—if anything at all—until he knew everything Neena had told her.

Since it was only early afternoon, she just needed to get their plan for tonight formulated and then she would still have time to get him talking about his dream and maybe even about his reaction to her working for the *Feiru* Liaison office. He had yet to bring it up and Sabrina wasn't going to go into a high stakes situations—like taking down Watkins at the school—until she was sure they could trust each other enough to work together.

She clenched her hands into fists to prevent herself from reaching for him and said, "Watkins is moving up the bombing of the school. According to Neena, he's going to do it tonight."

He crossed his arms over his chest. "Start from the beginning, and tell me everything Neena told you."

She did—well, everything except for one secret she'd promised to keep from Jorge—and when she finished, he looked her dead in the eye and said, "You've been doing this double-life thing for years, so I'm guessing you're good at telling whether someone is lying to you or not. What's your professional opinion on Neena? Imagine you had a team's life in your hands, would you still trust her and use her information?"

Sabrina had already given this a lot of thought. "Yes, I think she's telling the truth. Her eccentricities are genuine and I get the feeling that most people think she's lying because of them, when in reality she's being herself. It's kind of a brilliant cover, if you ask me. I wish I could just be myself and say whatever I wished, but then have people dismiss it out of hand because of my behavior. It'd be a hell of a lot easier than having to live two lives."

He uncrossed his arms. "About that, what made a human take an undercover job with the Fed League for two years? How long have you even known the *Feiru* existed?"

She hadn't meant to draw attention to her earlier revelations, but now that she had, she wouldn't try to brush them aside. "I sort of discovered your existence by accident."

He gave her a look and she decided they had enough time for her to tell him more. She hadn't told anyone outside of the *Feiru* Liaison office this story before, but if she wanted any sort of trust between them, she needed to stop worrying about what her superiors might do to her. Especially since her identity was already compromised.

She took a deep breath and said, "During my first year at university in Brazil, I was returning from a late night at the library. It was a clear, warm night, but all of a sudden I heard loud splashes of water, as if there was a downpour. I went toward the sound and came upon a young man surrounded by streams of water dancing around him, and occasionally one of the water streams would hit the ground. Like any human, all I could do was stare. The young man was standing in the open, and there was no logical reason I could think of for the displays of water—no fountain, no hoses, nothing.

"I didn't get to stare long, however, before I heard something like a gun go off. The young man went down, and the water instantly splashed against the ground to form a big puddle. As I tried to move away from the growing lake at my feet, arms grabbed my shoulders and spun me around. The woman was wearing a police-like uniform, but something about it was off."

Jorge said, "She was a *Feiru* enforcer."

Sabrina nodded. "Yes. I later learned they'd gotten a tip and had come to take care of the problem before someone could record the display of elemental magic with a camcorder or a video on their cell phone. The man was taken into custody, as was I."

"And what did they do with you?"

Despite everything she'd seen, and everything she'd experienced in her current occupation, that night was still the most important in her life because from that day onward, she'd never been able to be truly honest with anyone. Keeping it a secret from all of her friends and family, including her sister, had nearly torn her apart.

But with Jorge, she could finally break her silence, and maybe start to heal her fractured psyche. After all, he was a *Feiru*, and talking about the enforcer procedures wouldn't violate any of the agreements she'd signed. She might get in trouble with her boss back at the *Feiru* Liaison office, but she could handle that.

Besides, it was more than wanting to tell someone; she needed to tell someone. "At first, nothing. They kept me locked up and wouldn't tell me why. I couldn't even make a call to my sister to let her know I was alive. The thought of her and my friends thinking I was dead was one of the lowest points of my life."

Jorge took a step closer to her and briefly touched her arm. "They must've let you out eventually, or you wouldn't be standing here in front of me."

He was looking at her, his face almost soft like it had been in the old days, and she wanted him to touch her again. "They would occasionally question me to try to find out what I knew. Eventually, a *Feiru* lawyer came and explained my options to me—I could either spend the rest of my life in a special type of relocation center, or I could agree to work with the *Feiru* Liaison office as a type of spy. Since I could still see my sister occasionally with the latter option as long as I didn't tell her anything related to the *Feiru* or my new job, I chose that one."

Jorge was less than a foot in front of her now. She had to look up to see his face, but his expression was unreadable. This close, she could smell the unique masculine scent that was Jorge, but he didn't touch her or reach for her. Instead, he asked, "How old were you when this happened?"

"It happened a little over five years ago, when I was eighteen."

He lifted a hand and cupped her cheek. Her heart rate picked up and she barely resisted turning her head into his touch, afraid she might scare him away. Right now, she wanted comfort. Talking about her past and how bad luck had changed the course of her life forever was taking a toll on her emotions.

In addition to that, the strain of never sharing why she'd been forced to leave university had finally been eased, but if she wasn't careful, she might start to cry.

Jorge's voice was low when he said, "So, you understand what it's like to live a life not of your choosing."

She nodded, and he lifted his other hand to trace her cheek, the touch sending shivers down her spine. She searched his eyes and she said, "No one deserves to be forced into doing something the way you or I have. Do you believe me now, when I say I never would've shared your shadow-shifting secret if I'd known it would end up harming you?"

He nodded. "But in a way, it worked out for the best. If I'd never been forced to work for the Collector, you never would've told me your secret, and I never would've been able to do this."

He lowered his head and kissed her.

CHAPTER ELEVEN

Jorge knew he should be focusing on Watkins and finishing this job, but as Sabrina told him about how she'd been snatched at eighteen and forced to live a life not of her choosing, the last of his doubt about her dissolved. She may have had better conditions than he'd had with the Collector, but at least he'd been twenty-five when it'd happened to him. Sabrina had barely been an adult, and yet she'd taken her new circumstances and ran with them. An average human might've resented their new life, but instead, Sabrina had worked hard, resulting in the smart and talented woman in front of him.

Deep down, knowing she understood what it was like to do things you didn't want to do, made him want her more than ever. Out of everyone, Sabrina might understand and forgive the awful acts he'd committed to protect his sister.

And once he realized that, a loneliness he'd been denying all along finally came rushing forth. He wanted her, and he wanted her now.

Time was short, and even if the Collector found him tomorrow, he wanted to be with Sabrina at least once. They had until this evening to formulate a plan. Neena had said nothing about them needing to run or move until then, so Jorge was going to seize what might be his only chance with Sabrina. He lowered his head and kissed her.

He brushed his lips against hers, and again, desperate for her to respond. A second passed and then Sabrina placed her hands on his chest, grabbed onto his shirt, and nipped his lower lip.

He growled and moved his hands from her face to her back and pulled her flush again him. Sabrina gasped, but since she didn't make a move to stop him, he kissed her again and pushed his tongue into her mouth.

As she tangled her tongue with his, he squeezed her ass before rocking her hips against him, the friction making his hard cock even harder. When she dug her nails in his chest through his shirt, all he could think about was her nails raking his back.

He tried to maneuver them toward the bed, but Sabrina broke their kiss and pushed him away. Her strength was no match for his, but he released her. He had done some horrible acts, but forcing a woman wasn't one of them.

It took a second for Sabrina to catch her breath, and Jorge said, "What's wrong? I can tell you want this as much as me."

"Yes, but—" He reached for her, but Sabrina took a step back and shook her head. "Not now. Believe me, it's been a long time and I'd like nothing more than for you to fuck me until I forget my name, but not until after we take down Watkins."

"It's only early afternoon. We have plenty of time."

"It's not only that—I don't want you to sleep with me because you feel sorry for me. Give the air some time to clear, and if you still want me after tonight, you can have me."

He growled. "I've wanted you for nearly two years, Sabrina Ono. Believe me; I don't want you because of pity."

~~*

SHADOW OF TEMPTATION

Sabrina stared at the sexy, growling man in front of her and wanted nothing more than to run over and jump him. But she had a gut feeling that this wasn't the time or place to do this. Jorge now knew things about her that no one else did, and she wanted a chance with him, but if they didn't leave this place soon, she had a feeling something bad would happen.

The tough part was trying to convince the horny man in front of her that she wanted him more than anything she'd wanted in a long time, but just not right this second.

She decided laying out the facts would probably be the easiest way to distract him. "It's not only that, but I have a bad feeling about this place. If Neena knew about it, who else might? I don't know a whole lot about *Feiru* latent abilities, but is there one that can find us?"

Jorge ran a hand through his hair. "Shit, that depends. If Watkins has anything you've recently worn or touched, he can find us."

"I'm sure he does, but how can that lead him to us?"

Jorge snapped into work mode and started gathering things from the nightstand and other drawers in the room. "There's a latent ability called a 'Locator'. It's incredibly rare, but any *Feiru* with that ability can touch something you've recently worn or used and get a general sense of your current location." He tucked a gun into his back waistband. "I only worked with Luciana once, but as far as I know, she's still alive. She's a Locator and one of the biggest prizes the Collector has in her possession."

Sabrina pushed away the five hundred questions racing through her head and focused on the most important. "But even if we run, won't they just take something from here and find us again?"

Jorge faced her. "A person has to have touched the item with their skin in the last twenty-four hours. That time limit should be up soon for anything in your apartment, which means if we torch this place, they won't have any new leads."

She blinked. "You want to set this place on fire?"

He shrugged. "The houses in this area are abandoned. As long as we get someone to call the Merida fire department right away, they'll be able to contain it and we'll be able to make a clean run."

There was always a risk when fire was involved since it was unpredictable, but she trusted Jorge's judgment. Besides, in the crazy world of *Feiru* magic, it wasn't like they had any other choice. "Okay, let's do it your way. I'll just need a few minutes."

Sabrina started to gather her gun and a few other items—wallet, extra bullets, her new burner phone. When she had what she needed, she asked, "So, how are we going to do this?"

Jorge reached into a cupboard in the small kitchen and pulled out a tin jug of turpentine. "With this. Wait outside for me. I'll be there in a minute."

She nodded and stepped out. Jorge had worked with arson fires before, in the Fed League, and she trusted him to set it off without killing himself.

It was odd to think the Fed League had taught them something useful.

While she waited, she kept an eye on any pedestrians and tried to digest what Jorge had told her about yet another latent ability. A Shadow-Shifter, a Night-Weaver, a Locator—just how many abilities were there? And why hadn't her office trained her on how to deal with any of them?

If she managed to get out of this alive, and one of the higher-ups inside the *Feiru* Liaison office would listen, Sabrina was going to suggest some serious changes on how they not only trained recruits, but also on how they should work with the *Feiru* to root out those who possessed latent abilities. Without someone educating the *Feiru* on how to protect themselves against people like the Collector, some very 'bad yet powerful people' could make the world a whole lot worse.

She heard the whoosh of a rapidly set fire, and Jorge darted out a second later. He continued down the street and she followed him. She asked the first person they passed to call the fire department, and tried not to think about how much her life could change in the next few hours—for better or worse.

~~*

Jorge looked through his binoculars and surveyed the school perimeter before leaning in close to Sabrina. His intention was to whisper in her ear, but he couldn't help but take a deep inhale of her scent. Crouching next to her for over an hour, but being unable to touch her except for a casual brush of his shoulders now and then, had been agony. He was well aware of the stakes and how they needed to succeed, but for once, he regretted being a man. Sabrina looked cool and collected while he was losing a never-ending battle with a hard-on.

Focus, Salazar. He needed to live if he wanted to undress Sabrina and explore every inch of her body. For the first time, he had something to live for past rescuing his sister.

With his new goal in mind, he finally whispered, "Still no sign of him. Are you absolutely positive that Neena was telling the truth?"

She glanced at him and nodded. She was about to whisper something back when he heard some rustling. It was faint, but since it was a windless night, it meant he needed to investigate the sound. He looked through his binoculars and noticed a shadow that was too big to be a cat or dog. After lowering his binoculars, he put a finger to his lips and signaled that he would check out the noise while Sabrina stayed here to cover him.

She nodded in understanding and he slowly made his way down the street. He was careful to keep himself hidden behind the cars, until he could cross the street out of the sight line of the shadowy figure. Since it was nearly midnight, the streets were empty in this part of the city. He crossed without being seen and crept between the trees and the school wall. As he drew closer, the shadow he assumed was a person was loud enough in its movements that a person walking on the street could hear it. That told him that the shadow he'd spotted wasn't Watkins.

Still, he wasn't taking any chances. It wasn't beneath Watkins to use a teenage troublemaker as a decoy to draw them out.

He was soon close enough that he could make out some of the woman's features in the faint glow of the streetlights—short, curly hair and dark skin. If he were to hazard a guess, it was Luciana Ribeiro, the Collector's Locator.

To protect her, Luciana had always been kept away from the front lines in past operations. Something about her presence here was off.

He kept his gun in his hand and rushed her. When he reached her, he placed his free hand over her mouth and pressed the muzzle of his gun into her side. He whispered, "I'm going to remove my hand and ask you some questions. If you make a sound above a whisper, I'll shoot you, Luciana. Understand?"

Since Luciana wasn't trained for combat like Jorge, she nodded as he had predicted she would. He continued. "You're a Locator and shouldn't be here. Tell me why you are."

He kept his finger just outside the trigger and removed his hand. Thankfully, she didn't scream but instead whispered, "I want to know how you got out."

That wasn't the answer he'd been expecting. "Is this a stalling tactic?" He gave a quick look around. "I don't see anyone, but that doesn't mean they aren't there." He pressed his gun harder into her side. "Now, stop with the games and tell me the truth."

"But I am telling the truth. They used to keep my husband as 'encouragement' to keep me cooperative, but he disappeared. I'm not supposed to know, but I do. I want out so I can find him again before they do."

"If that's true, and your husband disappeared, he's probably dead."

She shook her head. "No, I refuse to give up. I know he's alive. He has a valuable set of skills."

"A latent ability?"

"No, but just as valuable."

Her tone was final, and he could tell she wasn't going to elaborate. Since he didn't have time to waste on such nonessential information, he decided to push on. "Let's pretend all of this is true. That still doesn't explain why you're here, alone, when you're supposed to be tracking me."

She looked at him over her shoulder. "They gave me thirty minutes to walk and clear my head of the others' influences. You know how my abilities work—sometimes having another person too close will affect my ability to track. And before you ask, I found something you dropped back at the place you torched."

That gives you two choices—help me and I can put the others off long enough for you to get Watkins, which I know where he is, by the way. Or, I can make noise and draw the others here, and you'll have to shoot me."

Judging by the defiant look in Luciana's eyes, she meant it.

Fuck. He didn't have a whole lot of choice in the matter. He could knock her unconscious, but then the others with her would come searching when she didn't check in.

He had zero right promising anything, but he was going to try. It was the best chance he and Sabrina had. "How I got out is complicated, but all I can do is try to help you. After you give me the info about Watkins, I need you to go back and pretend to find me. If all of this goes off without a hitch, and you don't betray me, I'll find a way to contact you and get you out."

"And I'm supposed to believe you, why?"

"Listen, I don't have time to argue. I'm the best chance you have for getting free of the Collector, so take it or leave it."

She stared at him and finally said, "Give me a piece of your shirt as collateral, and I'll agree. That way if you don't contact me within the next twenty-two hours, I'll have two hours to locate you, find you, and turn you in to the Collector's people."

Chapter Twelve

Sabrina had agreed to trust Jorge, but as they finished surveying the old shop across the street, she still felt uneasy about his deal with the Locator woman. Sabrina had known nothing about the Collector last week, but from what little she did know now, she was starting to put together a profile of both the woman and the people who worked for her. It wouldn't be out of line to assume Luciana was playing Jorge to protect her husband.

She shifted her position on the roof of an abandoned building and turned toward Jorge. "The windows are dark, and I don't see any movement. Are you sure about this? We only have one shot; Watkins won't let himself fall vulnerable again."

"I think Neena told us to go to the school so that we'd find Luciana, probably so she could try and get yet another person to help her organization by trading favors." He glanced at her. "Given the nature of your work, I gather you've spent years profiling people. Do you agree this fits what you know of Neena?"

At least Jorge was referring to her past and identity in a positive light. "It's possible, but the woman isn't exactly predictable."

"Do you have any other ideas?"

"No."

He reached out and brushed her cheek with his knuckles. "Then that's settled. The sooner we can finish this, the sooner you and I can talk about what happens next."

She felt a sudden rush of happiness at the prospect of Jorge wanting a future with her. They had issues—lots of issues—to work out and discuss, but the thought of being herself again focused her. "Okay, then we'll stick to the plan. When should your DEFEND friends arrive?"

Jorge had mentioned two *Feiru* named Santos and Jimenez organizing a team of DEFEND soldiers to help them. The phone call had been brief on their way here, but he seemed confident they would help out.

He nodded to the east. "The group in charge of the distraction should be there already, and the others should be in position near the shop. When the distraction is ready and the others are in place, the group in the east will signal us with a high-powered flashlight."

She looked toward the east, but all she saw were streetlights. Good, that meant she had at least a little more time to say what she needed to say. "Jorge." He looked back to her face. "Promise me that whatever happens, you won't kill Watkins outright and will hand him over to the *Feiru* enforcers."

"What makes you think I'd kill him?"

"Well, it's more than likely that he's the one who turned you over to the Collector."

Jorge fell silent for a second before glancing to the east and saying, "You put that together too, huh? Well, as much as I'd like to kill the bastard for the pain and suffering he's caused all of the *Feiru* he's handed over to the Collector, there's a reason why I can't."

"Why?"

Shadow of Temptation

"Because then I'd never get a chance with you."

~~*

The words slipped out before Jorge could stop them. This wasn't the time or place to get sentimental, but it was true—if he killed Watkins, then he'd probably be locked up and sent to some AMT research facility. Just because the *Feiru* High Council hadn't passed a law requiring all *Feiru* with latent abilities to be turned over to the AMT system didn't mean it wouldn't happen.

Hell, he had no idea if surviving tonight would result in anything with Sabrina, but dammit, he wanted to try.

Sabrina was staring at him with her mouth slightly open, but before either of them could say another word, there was a series of light flashes from the east. He switched into work mode. "Okay, that's the signal. Let's go."

Sabrina managed to close her mouth and nod.

The signal meant they had five minutes to climb down the one story building to the ground and get into position, and all without making a sound. At the edge of the roof, he eased over the side until his feet touched on the discarded sofa. Once he was down and out of the way, Sabrina did the same. They circled around the building and kept to the shadows to reach their target.

Ninety seconds to go. Most of the DEFEND soldiers would guard the back door, Sabrina the front, and Jorge would cover the door of the building adjacent to the shop where Watkins and the others assembling the bomb for the school would be. If what Sabrina had told him about Watkins was true, the man usually kept an empty dummy house or shop next door to his workshops or safe houses. He had a feeling Watkins would use the dummy house to escape.

109

However, Jorge wasn't an idiot and wouldn't go into this without sufficient backup. Luciana had mentioned other Fed League soldiers and maybe even a few latent abilities in there with Watkins. Just in case, a few DEFEND soldiers were keeping lookout from nearby rooftops, armed with rifles that shot tranquilizer darts.

Everyone was in position by the time a loud boom sounded from the east. Jorge hugged the shadows of the nearby wall, his gun out and ready. He might not be in his shadow form, but his black clothes hid him well enough.

The plan was for Santos to throw a homemade smoke bomb into the house and force the people inside to flee. If the human police somehow caught word of the smoke bombing, they would pin the homemade device on some of the local teenagers. The last thing they needed was the human police sniffing around and looking for DEFEND or the Fed League.

He heard some glass break and a few seconds later there were cries and coughs from near the back door of the original building, but he held his position. Anyone who'd done mercenary work as long as Watkins had would know that dividing his resources would also divide an enemy's. Sometimes the maneuver was a death sentence, other times the sole means of escape. Since Watkins only cared about himself, he'd divide his resources and not give a shit who else died.

A few more seconds passed, but while the front and back of the other house grew noisier with scuffling and the muffled sound of an occasional tranquilizer gun going off, nothing happened on his end.

Part of him itched to go help the others, but he trusted Sabrina and—oddly—Santos. DEFEND had yet to fuck him over, and if this went according to plan, he might even consider helping them out again if they asked him.

A window opened on his side of the building and a small amount of smoke started to trail outside. An arm and head poked out to look around, but it was just one of the Fed League lackeys. However, the lackey in question was one of Watkins's best bodyguards who just happened to be a dead shot.

The presence of the bodyguard meant Jorge was going to have to shift and use his shadow-transport trick to anonymously deliver Watkins to the *Feiru* enforcement agents in the area.

Jorge tucked his gun into his waistband and imagined his cells breaking down until the familiar pain shot through his body and he became a dense shadow-mist. He kept to the shadows as the lackey slipped out of the window and motioned one of his guns—he had two—to signal the all clear. As Watkins started to climb out the window, Jorge moved closer.

He'd never brushed up against someone to try to knock them unconscious before since all of his past assignments had been to get in and out as quickly as possible. This time, however, he was going to try.

The instant Watkins touched his feet on the ground, Jorge moved as fast as he could toward the lackey, brushed over him, and was relieved that the man fell down to the ground in unconsciousness. Watkins started to run, but in this form, Jorge was faster. He caught up with him and surrounded him from behind. Watkins also fell to the ground unconscious. As much as he didn't want to bring the bastard into his shadow cloud, Jorge knew he had to do it, so he started to imagine the bastard's cells breaking down. But just before he managed to finish the process, a sharp pain shot through him and he lost his concentration. One second he was a shadow cloud, and the next he was in his human form again.

What the fuck? Jorge glanced down his body and saw a knife sticking out of his thigh.

No one should've been able to hit him in his shadow form, but he didn't have time to figure out how it happened because something glowing light blue was charging straight at him.

The blue blur meant that Watkins had borrowed a *Feiru* with a latent ability called a Blue Demon from the Collector. He needed to stop the woman from reaching him, or it was game over since one of the Blue Demons' abilities included poison-filled claws.

He reached for his gun and aimed, but before he could pull the trigger, his hand dematerialized and rematerialized. The flash from skin to shadow and back again sent enough pain through his body to cause him to scream. The gun clattered to the ground, and the woman drew closer. But just before she reached him, Jorge heard a rifle and the woman went down.

In the back of his brain, he knew it was a tranquilizer dart, but before he could do anything, his arm flashed again, and he gritted his teeth against the pain. Something was wrong with him. Really wrong.

People started to come from all sides, but Jorge concentrated on his arm. If he couldn't get the flashing to stop, he was going to burn out and die.

He heard a female's voice and he looked up to see Sabrina. The split-second distraction cost him, because in that instant, he couldn't prepare against his body turning to shadow and back, and the pain was so overwhelming that he screamed before the world went black.

Shadow of Temptation

~~*

Sabrina had just finished securing the last of the unconscious Fed League people on her side of the building when one of the DEFEND soldiers came rushing up to her and said, "Something has happened to Salazar."

The person assisting her nodded for her to go and Sabrina stood up and ran to the far side. Her heart was already beating fast from the takedown, but her heart rate kicked up a notch as she rounded the corner. She refused to think Jorge could be dying, but as she saw his arm and a section of his torso flash into shadow and back to solid flesh, her stomach dropped. Something was wrong.

She kneeled by his side and gave him a quick once-over. While the knife in his leg would hurt like hell, it wasn't life threatening. She wanted to touch him and comfort him, but the switching between shadow and flesh stopped her. Until she knew exactly what was wrong with him, she couldn't risk making the situation worse.

"Jorge? What happened?" He looked at her and then he screamed in agony before his eyes closed and he went slack. Isabel Santos kneeled down across from her. Sabrina looked to the woman and said, "You know more about latent abilities than I do. What's wrong with him? If he keeps doing this, he'll burn out and he'll die."

Santos's face went grim. "I don't know what's wrong with him. Some of my people are trying to find someone who does."

Sabrina watched as Jorge's arm flashed again to shadow and back. It seemed unconsciousness didn't give him any kind of relief.

The man had already been through so much pain. He didn't deserve this. Her eyes started to water, but she caught herself and took a deep breath. Emotions could kill in the heat of a takedown. She needed to focus if she wanted to give Jorge the best chance at living.

She looked at Santos. "Since Jorge can't anonymously drop Watkins at the door of a local *Feiru* enforcer's office, we're going to need to think of something else. Can any of your people manage it?"

Santos shook her head. "DEFEND is technically an illegal organization. Some enforcers are lenient as long as we don't blatantly break any laws in front of them, but the enforcers in Merida are sticklers. Our best bet is for you to call your office and have them cart Watkins off."

Her heart skipped a beat. "How do you know about my office?"

Santos's gaze was steady. "Because I needed to know. Don't worry, I'm not going to out you. You helped my people, and for that, you've earned some respect."

Sabrina looked down at Jorge. She had planned to run with him after turning in Watkins. It wasn't much of a plan, but it would've given them time to try to find her a way out of being relocated by her boss.

But that plan had been replaced with a new one. She needed to give Santos time to try to find a way to stop the random shifting, which meant she was going to have to call her boss to clean up this mess. She'd have to stay until they arrived to make sure Watkins didn't get away. No doubt they'd lock her up afterward, once they discovered her cover had been blown.

As much as she wanted her freedom, Jorge's life was more important. She had no other choice but to sacrifice what future she might've had with him in order to save him.

She looked back up at Santos. "Can you give me your word that you'll look after him?"

Santos nodded. "I'll oversee his transport myself, and I'll find a way to contact you once we know what's wrong with him."

Sabrina was more aware of what wasn't being said rather than what was—Santos couldn't guarantee he'd live, but she'd let Sabrina know what happened regardless.

Of course, if Sabrina contacted her office, it was more than likely they'd relocate her and she'd never know what happened to Jorge. But if it meant Jorge at least had a chance, she would do it.

She nodded and pulled out her burner cell phone. Before she dialed, she said, "You might want to start getting your people out of here. The *Feiru* Liaison office will probably arrest all of you if given the opportunity."

Santos nodded and motioned some people over to where Jorge was lying on the ground. Sabrina waited until he flashed back to flesh before she risked caressing his cheek and said, "You'd better survive, Jorge Salazar. I have a thing or two to discuss with you."

Santos gave her an apologetic look and said, "Sabrina, we need you to move so we can try to transport him."

She gave one last long look at Jorge and nodded before she stood up and moved to a quiet corner away from the noise of the DEFEND soldiers' retreat. She kept Watkins in her sight—he was still unconscious with his hands secured behind his back with plastic ties—and watched as Santos and the others fashion a stretcher out of an old blanket. Thankfully, the blanket didn't turn into shadow when he did. The next time she saw Jorge—she *would* see him again—she'd have to ask him about that.

When Santos and her team hoisted Jorge up and walked away, Sabrina turned on her phone and dialed her boss's number.

It had been foolish to hope, but it looked like Neena's promise to keep her from being relocated had been a lie.

CHAPTER THIRTEEN

Jorge's eyes popped open as he drew in a deep gasp. Bright lights. Pain. Noise.

Everything jumbled together inside his head, and he tried to concentrate. But the pain coursing through every nerve in his body was so overwhelming a part of him just wanted to die. He'd do just about anything to make it go away.

Isabel Santos's face came into view and she frowned down at him and said, "I need you to stay awake and concentrate for me. After the next partial shift, we're going to try to remove the knife in your thigh. We think that is what's causing your uncontrollable shifting."

"How can a—" He flashed from flesh to shadow and back again. The pain was worse than he remembered from before, but somehow he managed not to scream.

When he was solid again, he managed between pants to say, "I can't take much more of this. Let me go back to sleep. Please."

"I'd never thought I'd see you ask for anything nicely, but no, you can't. Whatever substance coats that knife will probably kill you. The sooner we get it out, the sooner we can try to neutralize the effects."

He wondered how she knew so much about medicine, but a different realization hit him. "Where's Sabrina? Is she safe?"

Santos nodded. "She's fine. And if you ever want to see Sabrina Ono again, you're going to do as I say."

A small sense of relief flooded him, but then he felt another shift coming on and he focused on that. "It's going to happen again. Tell me what to do."

"Okay. Right after the shift, use every bit of energy you have to keep yourself solid. It's imperative that we get the knife out of you to keep you alive. After all, you can't get into Ono's pants if you're dead."

He wanted to flip his middle finger, but he wasn't about to waste what precious energy he had, so he let it go. He could piss off Santos later.

He let the shift happen and clenched his jaw against the pain. As soon as he was flesh again, he used every last bit of his energy to imagine himself solid. He could feel his body wanting to break down, but he pushed it back. He wanted to see Sabrina again and to do that he needed to live.

Someone started pulling the knife out of his leg. The pain was unlike anything he'd ever experienced, as if someone were squeezing his heart with a clamp; he gripped the sheets with his hands as he groaned through his clenched teeth. Once the blade was free, the driving need to shift his body into shadow lessened at the same time as an excruciating flash of pain coursed through his body. Before anyone in the room could say a word, the world went dark again.

~~*

Sabrina stared out the sole window in her room and wondered for the thousandth time if Jorge was still alive. After her phone call back at the takedown site, her boss had taken Watkins and led a team to bust the other high-ranking members

118

of the Fed League scattered across Mexico. For all intents and purposes, the Fed League was no more, at least in Mexico.

She should take some satisfaction in knowing that her undercover assignment had been a success, but unlike when she'd finished her job in Rio two years ago, Sabrina was anything but happy. And it wasn't just because of not knowing what had happened to Jorge.

The room where she sat might look like a hotel room, but in reality, it was her prison cell. She'd been sequestered here for the last two days while the higher-ups decided what to do with her since her identity had been compromised. True, Watkins and the Fed League in the area were gone, but the mysterious Collector woman was a constant threat. Especially since the *Feiru* Liaison office had never heard of her before Sabrina's report.

In all likelihood, she would soon be relocated. She'd never be able to see Jorge or her sister ever again.

The lock clicked and her door opened to reveal one of the rookie *Feiru* Liaison officers who'd been assigned as her guard. She'd seen his face around before he'd become her guard, but she didn't know his name, and since she didn't really care, she hadn't asked.

The man motioned for her to come and said, "Marquez and Garcia want to see you."

She stood up and followed the man down the hallway. Jose Garcia was the head honcho of the Mexico City office. No doubt they'd be telling her about her future today.

They arrived at one of the meeting rooms and her guard motioned her inside. Sabrina stepped into the room and nearly did a double take at who was sitting at the table. Marquez and Garcia were there, but so was Neena Chatterjee.

Neena gave her a small wave and said, "Come in, my dear." She motioned to the seat across from her. "I saved you a cookie."

Sabrina snapped out of her disbelief and took the seat. Sure enough, there was a cookie sitting on a napkin, but she wasn't hungry. Instead, she looked from Neena to Marquez to Garcia. DEFEND wasn't exactly a designated enemy, but neither was it an ally. She asked, "Anyone want to tell me what's going on here?"

Her boss, Marquez, gestured toward Neena. "Ms. Chatterjee here has been in deep talks and negotiations with us over the last two days, and we've come to an agreement."

She raised an eyebrow and couldn't help but be sarcastic. "Oh really. Did she promise to save the world? Or give you the information you need to catch one of your most wanted *Feiru* criminals?"

Marquez opened his mouth, but Neena beat him to it. "We have made a temporary agreement to work together. Someone is circulating nasty rumors about my organization, and I'm out to prove to Mr. Garcia here that the rumors aren't true."

"And what does this have to do with me?"

Neena waved for Garcia to tell her. The head of the *Feiru* Liaison office didn't look pleased at the gesture, but he looked at Sabrina and said, "We had originally slotted you to be relocated, to protect both you and our office. However, thanks to Ms. Chatterjee here, you have a second option."

Anything that involved working with Neena would be a headache, but it could give her a chance at freedom and finding out if Jorge was still alive. "What does it require me to do?"

Garcia looked to Neena, but she didn't say anything, so he continued. "You will be our trial go-between. You'll spend most of your time working with DEFEND—that will make it easier to hide your identity—but you will periodically report to Marquez, as well as take requests from him to pass on to Ms. Chatterjee and others inside DEFEND. Technically, you will still be working for me, but Ms. Chatterjee has the final say in what you can do and with whom you can interact with."

Neena Chatterjee in charge of her life. Fantastic. "And what happens if the temporary trial period doesn't go well? What happens to me then?"

Garcia spoke up. "You'll have the option to resign from our employ and work for DEFEND permanently, provided you sign a nondisclosure agreement and take a new identity. Or, you can be relocated with other outed agents. However, if you choose to stay with DEFEND, we will no longer be able to protect you. If DEFEND does something illegal, you'll be as liable as every other person involved."

Sabrina looked to Neena. The woman was folding some kind of origami figure. "Neena, before I agree to anything, what happened to Jorge?"

Neena finished her paper crane with a flourish and smiled. "Say yes, and I'll take you to him."

Marquez said, "We haven't processed the necessary paperwork and—"

Neena interrupted him. "You and your paperwork. Sabrina has been doing a bang-up job at keeping it together. Let her see her fellow and make sure he's okay."

Sabrina's two superiors gave her looks, but she kept her shoulders straight and expression calm. They wouldn't shame her for falling for a *Feiru*. "Before I sign anything, I have a few suggestions I want you to implement, but I'm in." She looked to Neena. "Now, take me to see Jorge."

Jorge tried to concentrate on the movie on the TV in his room, but the distraction wasn't working—he kept thinking about Sabrina.

Santos and the others watching over him refused to let him out of this room. They kept saying stuff like, "We need to monitor your vitals" or "We need to keep running blood tests." Yet when he asked them about Sabrina, they would suddenly shut up and mutter something about Neena would tell him about her when she was ready.

A small part of him was afraid that now the danger and heat of the moment had cooled down, Sabrina didn't want to see him. But remembering the feel of her in his arms, kissing him, or how he'd heard of her sacrifice to turn Watkins over to the authorities instead of running away with him for a chance at freedom, he knew that no matter what she felt for him, she would confront him if given the chance.

He still couldn't believe she risked giving up her future so that Santos and the other could whisk him away to safety. He owed her his life.

Hell, she'd saved his life before that when she'd given him a reason to live. Because of Sabrina, he'd been able to rescue Luciana. Who knew how many other people he could help simply because one woman had found a way into his heart.

He turned off the TV. All of this thinking and wondering was making him soft, and he wasn't sure he liked it.

Someone approached the glass window next to his door. Then Santos—who he'd learned had been a nurse before joining DEFEND—entered his room and looked at the machines hooked up to him. "Everything looks good. I think we've flushed the chemical cocktail that was causing your uncontrollable shifting out of your system. Just in time for your visitors, too."

He'd only been half-listening up to that point, but at the word "visitors" he looked to Santos. He was careful not to let his hope show on his face. "Who?"

"Neena and her friend."

And his hope died. If Sabrina had accompanied Neena, not even Santos was cruel enough to keep that from him. "The last time I saw Neena, she drugged me. I don't trust her. Do I have the option of getting security in here to watch over me?"

Santos rolled her eyes. "Somehow I don't think you'll want security in here with you."

He was about to ask her to clarify when Neena walked into the room. Alone.

Jorge decided bluntness was his best strategy. "If you're here to talk me into working for your organization, the answer will be 'no' until you let me see Sabrina."

Neena waited for Santos to leave before she said, "Are you certain she wants to see you?"

For a second, he doubted himself, but then he pushed it away. "Of course she does. Now, stop with your games and get to why you're here. Then we can talk about letting me out of this damn room."

Neena clicked her tongue as she placed her hands on the chair next to his bed and leaned forward. "I think Sabrina's first assignment is to condition you to some manners. I'm sure she can think of some creative ways to get you to say please."

He blinked. "What the hell are you talking about?"

Neena smiled. "Your new partner, of course."

"My new partner?"

"Really, my dear, did that drug mess with your mind as well as your latent abilities? I know that your shadow-shifting abilities may never return, but let's hope your brain does, or you'll be next to useless."

When Jorge had learned his abilities might not return, he'd felt a mixture of relief and sadness. But if what Neena was saying were true, and he'd be working with Sabrina, then the lack of his abilities might endanger her life. Would she not want him anymore? After all, she'd never responded to his advances when he'd been without his abilities.

Neena's words interrupted his thoughts. "Let her decide."

He narrowed his eyes. "How do you do that?"

"It's none of your concern. What I need you to do is open the drawer next to your bed, take out the clipboard, read it, and sign it. Once Santos collects it, I'll let you see Sabrina."

Before he could say anything else, Neena turned and walked out of the room.

CHAPTER FOURTEEN

Sabrina uncrossed and crossed her legs before she started tapping her fingers against her thigh. She'd spent the last hour in this apartment of rooms waiting for Neena, and she didn't know how much longer she could keep her promise not to go wandering. Even with two guards at the door, she was contemplating the best way to escape.

Especially since she'd been told that Jorge was in the same building.

She kept replaying the scene when he'd told her that he wouldn't kill Watkins because then he'd never have a chance with her. Jorge finally tamping down his revenge for her sake meant more to her than she'd ever imagined. He might've changed because of his time with the Collector, but the sensitive man he'd once been hadn't completely died. He was still in there, and she wanted to know both the old and new versions of Jorge.

She stood up and started pacing the living area. After living so many years undercover and hiding her true self, not being able to see the one man with whom she could be honest was killing her. What was taking Neena so long?

There was a knock on the door and she frowned. Neena usually barged in without waiting, so it had to be someone else.

She stood up, walked over to the door, and opened it to find Jorge standing in front of her in a hospital gown. He studied her and Sabrina noticed how he looked a little pale with circles under his eyes, but the direct stare assessing her meant that while his body might be recovering, his mind was intact.

Relief flooded her, and she wanted nothing more than to pull him close and kiss him, but she was aware of the guards in the hall. She didn't want an audience, so she grabbed Jorge's arm, pulled him inside, and shut and locked the door. She took a deep breath and turned around to face him. Any doubts she had about him still wanting her instantly died at the heat in his eyes.

She barely managed a breathless, "Hi," before Jorge pressed her up against the door, his hands on either side of her face. His breath was hot against her cheek when he said, "I know we have a shitload of things to talk about, but right now, all I want to do is kiss you, get you naked, and show you just how glad I am that you're alive." He nuzzled her cheek. "Will you let me do that?"

Her heart thudded in her ears as Jorge pressed his lower body against hers. Whatever his recovery, she could feel he was hard and ready for her.

She wanted that hardness inside her, to remind her that he was alive, and that he was hers. She placed her hands on his chest and whispered, "Yes. Now, shut up and kiss me."

He growled, took her face into his hands, and did as she commanded. She opened in response to his touch, and welcomed the taste and warmth of Jorge's tongue in her mouth.

She hugged his body close, snaking a hand up his neck and into his hair. Her already hard nipples pressed against his chest, and she suddenly ached to feel his skin against hers.

She ran her free hand along his back, found the seam of his hospital gown, and ran her fingers down to his ass. She squeezed his firm buttocks and broke the kiss long enough to say, "Bedroom. Naked. Now."

SHADOW OF TEMPTATION

~~*

Jorge had worried that his straightforward request for sex might offend Sabrina. However, judging by how she was rubbing herself up against him and grabbing his ass, she was just as hungry for him as he was for her.

Despite the battle of their tongues inside her mouth, he wanted more. He wanted her skin under his palm, her heat wrapped around his dick, and her moans filling his ears. He needed to be reminded that he was alive, and so was she.

When she made her blunt demands about getting naked in the bedroom, he was more than happy to comply.

He'd take care of the naked part first.

He moved his hands to the hem of her shirt and ran his palms underneath it, against her skin, until he came to the band of her bra. It took everything he had to break their kiss and step back enough to tug up her shirt. Sabrina raised her arms, and as soon as he tossed her top aside, she reached behind her and unhooked her bra. She yanked it off and his mouth went dry.

The brief time he'd seen her naked torso before hadn't been enough to truly appreciate her breasts. They were small but high and topped with hard, dusky nipples. While Sabrina was busy unzipping her jeans, he reached out and cupped them. The woman was determined, however, and didn't stop until her shoes and jeans were kicked off to the side. He decided to get her attention and pinched her nipples.

A soft moan escaped her lips as she looked up at him. Her eyes were half-lidded and full of heat. The thought of her parted lips, soft and wet, as she explored his body made his cock throb.

He rolled her nipples between his thumb and forefinger a second before he trailed his hands down her body, inch by inch, until he reached the waistband of her no-nonsense cotton underwear. He ran a finger under the elastic, her smooth skin warm and inviting. For the first time in a long time, he felt the urge to tease someone.

He smiled and said, "I see you came prepared to seduce me."

She frowned. "If you want fancy thongs, then I'm not your lady. The goods are the same underneath."

He knew it was cheesy, but he'd do whatever it took to get the woman naked faster. "Then hurry up and show me. You said the other day that I could lick you to orgasm, and I'm impatient to taste you."

She blinked and then slowly smiled before she pushed against his chest. "Take two steps back first."

"What?"

"Just do it."

Unsure of what she had planned, he reluctantly stepped back. The thought of her changing her mind had his heart thumping in his ears. He wanted her so bad it hurt.

Sabrina slowly slid down the waistband of her underwear to expose more of her hip, and his panic calmed. The woman was trying to strip—for him.

But just before she revealed the hair between her thighs, she paused and said, "I don't need a pair of fancy underwear to seduce you." She stepped to the side and walked around him, her hips swaying. "Just stand here until I reach the bedroom. Can you do that?"

He nodded, curious to see what she would do. He'd never seen this side of her before, but so far, he liked it.

Her smile broadened at his nod before she stepped out of her underwear and tossed them aside. He drank in the sight of her narrow hips, the dark patch of hair between her thighs, and miles of golden, tan skin. He let his gaze linger on her hips and breasts before looking back to Sabrina's almond-shaped eyes. She hadn't said anything about remaining quiet, and his voice was low when he said, "You're so beautiful, it hurts." He untied his hospital gown and shrugged out of it. As it fell to the ground, Sabrina's eyes fell to his cock. He took it in his hand and yanked up and then down before he said, "Hurry up and strut your fine self into the bedroom so I can fuck you until you forget your name."

He was afraid his blunt talk would scare her, but while her eyes widened at his words, her wicked smile never faltered. "Did you bring any condoms this time?"

His stomach dropped. "I've been stuck inside a hospital-type room for two days. What do you think?"

She strutted over to her jeans, turned, and bent over so that her heart-shaped ass was on display. At that moment, he just wanted to push her up against the wall and take her from behind.

Sabrina looked over her shoulder and held up a strip of condoms. "Do you think this is enough?"

He knew he'd made a promise to wait, but fuck it. He rushed over to Sabrina, put an arm around her waist, and pulled her soft-yet-firm ass up against his cock. "Unless you want a little Jorge running around in nine months, you'd better give me one of those. I'll lick you to insanity later. Right now, I need to be inside you."

~~*

Sabrina had no idea what had come over her, but apparently she'd discovered how much she liked teasing Jorge. No doubt the longer she wasn't undercover, the more she'd discover about her true self.

Then she pushed him too far, and he grabbed her from behind. She was now flush against his hard cock, his muscled arm just under her breasts. While she wanted to feel the heat of his mouth around her nipple or his wet tongue between her thighs, she had a growing need to have Jorge inside her. The thought of his hard cock pounding at her from behind made her core pulse. She wanted this more than anything she'd wanted in a long time, so she opened one of the condom packets and handed it to him.

He nuzzled her neck with his soft lips and kissed her before he released his hold on her. The tender gesture reminded her of the complex man Jorge had become. She could easily imagine him being rough and hard one minute, and tender and loving the next.

But then Jorge's hands covered her breasts and he gently pulled her back up against his chest. He nipped her earlobe before he whispered, "Brace your arms against the wall."

She leaned over and as soon as she braced her forearms on the wall, one of Jorge's hands slid from her breast to between her thighs. He stopped just shy of her clit and rubbed his finger back and forth, teasing her. "Are you nice and wet for me?"

His questions sent more wetness between her legs. "Yes."

He nipped her shoulder and said, "Let's find out."

He held her another second before he plunged one of his fingers inside her. She let out a little moan and Jorge added another one before he started to pump his fingers in and out. "So wet and tight." He removed his fingers and she raised her head to see him smiling.

She was about to ask him what was so funny when he thrust his hard cock inside of her, stretching and filling her in a way that caused a second of discomfort. Then he pulled out slowly and thrust again and the discomfort turned into pure pleasure, spreading from her core up through her body. As his thrusts became faster, Sabrina braced her head against her arms and closed her eyes, allowing her to concentrate on the fullness of Jorge's cock and the rough warmth of his hand fondling one breast and then another.

The loud slap of his flesh against hers nearly drowned out her moans.

Jorge let go of her breast and she made a sound of protest. He changed the angle of his cock, and her protests died as lights danced against the darkness of her closed eyelids.

His breath was hot against her ear as he whispered, "You're mine, Sabrina Ono. Say it."

She was so close. "Yes, I'm yours. Jorge, please."

He kissed the top of her ear as the hand that had been playing with her breasts slid down her belly. "As you wish."

The second he started to rub his rough fingers against her clit, Sabrina let go.

~~*

From the instant he'd driven his cock into her, it'd taken everything he'd had not to come. She was so hot and tight, gripping his cock in a way his hand never could. It felt fucking fantastic.

But it was more than just feeling good—Sabrina trusting him with her body kindled something inside of him. Not that long ago, he'd been broken and ready to give up his life once his sister had been safe. But now, thanks to the warm and willing woman in front of him, he had so much more to live for.

He knew their connection was new, and who the hell knew what would happen next, but he couldn't stop from saying Sabrina was his. When she agreed, his baser need to claim her took over.

After a few strokes of her clit, Sabrina's inner muscles started squeezing his cock, her already tight sheath getting tighter. He moved so that both of his hands gripped her hips, and he let his restraint go. He thrust hard and fast, the pressure building at the base of his spine until his own orgasm hit him and he grunted out in pleasure. He wanted to scream out Sabrina's name, but he didn't want to appear clingy. After his time with the Collector, expressing emotions was sometimes hard to do.

Once he came down from the high, he slowed his hips and gently kissed Sabrina's damp shoulder. He loved the saltiness of her skin, reminding him how he'd yet to lick every inch of her body. His cock liked that idea, but for once, his head overruled—it was time for them to talk.

Still, he couldn't resist leaning forward, wrapping his arms around Sabrina's waist, and resting his chin on her shoulder. He gave her a gentle squeeze and asked, "How was that for hello?"

She leaned her head against his and he could hear the smile in her voice. "It was good, but I think you could do better." She turned her head toward him. "Do you want to try again?"

He ran his thumb up and down her arm. "Believe me, I want to, but I think it's high time we talked."

She nodded with a sigh. "I had a feeling you were going to say that."

He gave a reassuring squeeze. "Hey, it's not like I'm just going to take you against the wall and walk away." He released her, slipped out of her body, and turned Sabrina toward him. "I plan to be around for a long while, and not just because we're supposed to work together."

She frowned. "Work together? What are you talking about?"

He took her hands and squeezed them. "Come. Let's clean up, and then I'll tell you everything."

Chapter Fifteen

Sabrina was simultaneously sore, relaxed, and anxious. Being taken from behind was definitely something she wanted to do many times over again in the future. Just remembering how deep Jorge had reached inside of her made her heart rate kick up.

But as good as the sex had been, now came the aftermath, which meant talking about very important and scary things.

She'd never had to worry about planning her own future before. For the last five years, she'd been given assignments and tasks, and did everything she could to finish them. True, she'd devised tactics and strategies for how to succeed, but she'd never really been in charge of her personal life, let alone been able to think about whom she might share it with.

She glanced toward the closed bathroom door where Jorge was cleaning up. Was there a future with him? She hoped so.

The door opened, and while she loved looking at the deep brown of his bare chest and arms, she was disappointed to see he'd donned a pair of boxers. It must've shown on her face because Jorge came over and stroked her cheek with his thumb. "Don't look so sad, Sabrina. The boxers are keeping me from taking you again, right here and now, because we need to square away a few things first. The faster we talk, the faster you can decide if you'll honor me with your body again."

Some of her anxiousness eased. "For all of your claims of the nicer version of Jorge Salazar being dead, that comment tells me some of him survived."

His smile faded. "If you're waiting for him to come back, it's not going to happen. I was rarely tortured outright, but being forced to kill to survive and protect those close to you is something that will change a person."

At the mention of him being tortured, Sabrina remembered the secret Neena had told her during their first chat; the one Sabrina had decided to keep from Jorge when she'd recounted all Neena had told her: *If he doesn't tell someone about his guilt and experiences from his time with the Collector, Jorge Salazar will die within the month.*

She'd dismissed it at the time, but after everything that happened and Neena's tendency to be right, she wasn't going to take any chances. Call her selfish, but she wanted Jorge to live. She was falling for him, and she wanted time to explore those feelings outside of a constant life or death situation.

Of course, getting Jorge to talk wasn't going to be easy, but she had to try. She patted the bed next to her. "The only Jorge Salazar I want is the man you are now. Now, sit down and keep me warm while you tell me about that nightmare from the other day."

He opened his mouth, but Sabrina beat him to it. "No, you're not going to deflect it this time, Salazar. If you want any sort of relationship with me—work or otherwise—then you're going to start being honest. If all I've told you about my past and who I am isn't enough to let you trust me, then walk away now because I'm not going to keep wasting my time proving over and over again that I'm not out to stab you in the back."

He simply said, "I know."

She hadn't expected that answer.

Hiding her surprise at his easy agreement, she patted the bed next to her. "Then sit your ass down and start talking."

~~*

Jorge sat next to Sabrina and pulled her close against his side. He kissed her hair and said, "A little bossy, aren't we?"

"Jorge, stop trying to deflect and—"

He moved to nuzzle her forehead. "You didn't let me finish. I like it when you're bossy."

She pushed against his chest and looked him dead in the eye. "Tell me about the nightmare or I'll put my clothes back on and stand on the far side of the room, where you can't touch me, if that's what it takes."

He sighed. Talking about his dreams and time with the Collector was the last thing he wanted to do. Especially because deep down, he was afraid Sabrina might not be able to forgive him for what he'd done.

A hand brushed his chest and he looked down. Sabrina's face was soft, and her eyes were full of encouragement. "You can tell me anything. You know about some of the stuff I've had to do to keep up my cover ID. I know what it's like to make the least evil of two bad choices."

"That's what people say to make themselves feel better." She narrowed her eyes. "Jorge."

Remember, you're not inside the Collector's facilities anymore. Sabrina won't hurt you for displaying any emotion other than strength and obedience.

He laid his head on top of hers. If he was going to do this, he didn't want to watch the horror creep into Sabrina's expression. "In the dream I had the other day, Watkins came into a room with my sister, slit her throat, and said I was no better than him. In a way, I believe it. I've killed or kidnapped innocents—fathers, mothers, someone's sister or husband—all to protect the life of my sister Alejandra. I would do it again to protect her, but I'm aware of how selfish it was to keep ruining people's lives to protect one person. If I were a better man, I might've realized the kidnappings, etc., would never end and I should've escaped to expose the Collector and her coerced army. But I wasn't strong enough to let my sister die."

He closed his eyes a second and then let out a sigh. "Don't you see? If I'd been strong enough, I could've saved hundreds, maybe even thousands, of humans and *Feiru*. But I didn't. You were able to give up everything—your life, your friends, hell, even admitting you're human—to help make the world a better place." He opened his eyes and decided he needed to stop being a chickenshit and see what Sabrina was thinking. He looked down at her face, but it wasn't disgust or disappointment he saw, but rather she was angry. "What's wrong?"

"Wanting to protect your family isn't selfish. Part of what I've done is for the same reason, to protect my sister. The other part was for far less noble reasons than what you've created in your mind." She turned her body toward him. "I didn't want to live a life of seclusion. If I'd chosen that path, no one would've been hurt and my sister still would've been safe. Yet I still chose the life with the *Feiru* Liaison office and all that went with it. So don't you go thinking I'm all noble and self-sacrificing, because I'm not. We've both done what we thought best at the time, and we've learned from it. The cowardly thing to do is to throw that knowledge away and simply give up. So are you going to keep living in the past, blaming yourself for what can't be changed, or are you going to try to make up for it by making the future better for those still alive?"

~~*

Sabrina was part angry, and part ashamed. She'd never admitted how selfish she'd been in her choice to join the *Feiru* Liaison office, but it was true. If she'd just allowed herself to be locked away, she wouldn't have blood on her hands.

But, screw that. She'd done good things too, and there was so much more she could do to help both the *Feiru* and the humans, especially if Jorge was at her side. She just needed to convince him to help her.

The corner of his mouth ticked up. "Now I'm going to have to prove I'm not a coward, aren't I?"

Her body relaxed a fraction. "As long as it doesn't mean you're going to start beating your chest and doing stupid stunts to prove your manliness."

His eyes were now at half-mast, and full of heat. "I'd rather prove my manliness in other ways."

Her mouth went dry at his husky tone, but she gave her head a shake and playfully slapped Jorge on the chest. "Stop it. You still haven't told me what you meant by us working as a team."

Jorge's look only grew more intense. Then one second she was sitting next to him, and the next, he'd flipped her onto her back on the bed. He moved and caged her body with his before he said, "We're going to be partners in DEFEND. We can hash out who's in charge later. Right now, I want to pleasure my girlfriend until she screams my name loud enough that the guards in the hall can hear her."

She stopped breathing. After so many years of wishing she could have someone to confide in, someone she could truly be herself around, she didn't want to hope she finally had a chance at happiness. The secret agent in her needed to know the unequivocal truth. "Girlfriend?"

He leaned his head down and nipped her jaw. "I want you so much it hurts. You've given me a second chance at life, and I don't plan on taking it for granted. My first act is to make you mine and show you how much I want you because the sex in the front room was barely icing on the cake to my feelings. So say yes, Sabrina, because I want to treasure you in the way you deserve."

Her heart was pounding in her ears, but she knew she'd heard him correctly. In that second, she knew she would keep fighting to make Jorge the man he could be. Given some time, he would accomplish some of those grand plans she'd heard all those months ago of how he would save the first-borns.

And she would be by his side.

She brushed the hair from his forehead and tucked it behind his ear. "As long as I can do a little 'treasuring' of you too, then my answer is yes."

He smiled. "Baby, you can do whatever you want to me as long as you promise not to cut off certain parts of my anatomy."

She laughed. "I can't make any promises, but I will try every other trick I have before it reaches that point."

As Sabrina stared into his dark brown eyes, she decided they'd done enough talking for now. She reached her hand up, threaded it through his shoulder-length hair, and pulled his head down to hers. "Now, kiss me to seal the deal."

Jorge lowered his head and kissed her gently. "Is that all you want?"

"Jorge."

He grinned and her heart skipped a beat. The man was gorgeous when he full-on smiled.

Jorge let his weight settled on top of her and he whispered into her ear, "Let's see if I can get you to say my name without the reproof, and much, much louder."

Before she could say a word, he kissed her and delved his tongue into her mouth. It wasn't long before he had his wish, and reproof was the farthest thing from what was on her mind.

EPILOGUE

Two weeks later in Bogotá, Colombia

Sabrina lay next to Jorge on top of a flat roof, looking through her binoculars at a dilapidated house two blocks down the hill. She was waiting for a signal, but the tall plant was still standing straight up. She lowered her binoculars. "How are they still not ready?"

He gently rammed her shoulder with his. "Give them some time. Not everyone is as punctual as you are."

"There is nothing wrong with being punctual. But this is my first time working with Cam and Marco, and so far I'm not understanding their 'don't fuck with us' reputation."

Jorge chuckled. "Just don't say that within hearing. According to Santos, Marco can do some crazy shit with his elemental powers, and from what I've heard, Cam isn't far behind, even without taking her latent ability into account."

She handed Jorge the binoculars, and he took his turn watching for the plant to be flipped on its side and covered with a white sheet. She studied his face. "Are you upset that you can't be down there with them?"

Jorge kept looking through the binoculars. "No."

"Jorge."

He sighed and looked at her. "Yes, it would be awesome if my shadow-shifting abilities had come back and I could sneak in to help save more lives, but I have other skills, too. Besides, that means I get to watch your back, my little human."

She clasped her hands in front of her. "Thank goodness I have my big, strong *Feiru* boyfriend to look after me." She rolled her eyes. "I came here as a favor to you, so how about you stop belittling my skills and go back to watching that damn plant."

But Jorge just continued to stare at her. She rubbed a hand over her cheek and said, "What? Do I have something on my face?"

He gave a lazy smile. "No, I just realized something."

"What? Did we forget to do something for the take-down?"

He shook his head and traced a finger down her cheek. "No, it just hit me how much I love you."

Her heart skipped a beat. She stared at him a second before glancing quickly to the building with the plant. She could just barely make out the shape—it was still standing up. She looked back at him. "You decided to tell me this now?"

He shrugged. "It seemed as good a time as any other."

Sabrina had fallen for him early, but had decided not tell him how she felt until he was ready. To say that Jorge was at high-risk for running was an understatement. The man was still working through his nightmares as well as still trying to display non-sarcastic emotions to anyone other than her.

But in all of her hopes and dreams of this moment, she hadn't imagined him saying he loved her while lying on a roof of a broken down building, waiting for the signal to help take down the Colombian arm of the Federation League.

Of course, his do-it-in-the-moment approach was just one of the many things she loved about him.

She grabbed his chin, turned his face toward hers, and kissed him gently. "I love you too, but if you think I'm going to reward you with sex right now, then you're sadly mistaken."

He grinned. "I'll take your rain check. It gives me another reason not to screw this up."

She gave him one more kiss and then turned his head back toward their target. "Good. Then go back to watching the plant."

"Yes, ma'am."

She shook her head. She might love him, but there were still times when he tried her patience. Of course, she wouldn't have it any other way. The last two weeks had been healing not just for him, but for her as well. Each day she seemed to realize more and more of who she was, and a large part of that was thanks to the man next to her.

"Sabrina, there's the signal. Move into position."

Her mind switched into work mode and she crawled over to the modified sniper rifle already loaded and ready for her. She gently moved behind it, peered through the scope and said, "Ready."

She couldn't see him, but she knew Jorge was giving the "We're ready here" signal.

Sabrina had practiced for hours over the last week to brush up on her rifle training from her rookie days as a *Feiru* Liaison officer, but she still took in a few slow, deep breaths to calm her nerves. This was her first real mission for her new DEFEND/*Feiru* Liaison office position. This needed to go well, or it could damage the fragile partnership.

She watched as Cam and Marco flushed out the building, and the Fed League members started to flee into the streets. Due to the roadblocks and other DEFEND soldiers, the few who managed to escape were heading her way. When they were close enough, she fired one tranquilizer round, and then another, until she had four unconscious people down on the street.

She kept her mind in the zone until she heard Jorge whisper, "That's it. It's over."

She moved away from the rifle and sat back on her legs. As she rotated her shoulders, Jorge took her chin in hand and lowered his face to kiss her. "The mission's over. Does that mean I get sex now?"

She laughed, and any remaining tension she'd had from the operation eased. "I guess men really do only have one thing on their minds."

Jorge grinned and pulled her flush up against him. "I can't help it. Seeing you at that rifle, damn, Sabrina, you were sexy as hell."

"I had to show you that I don't need a strong, muscled *Feiru* boyfriend to take care of me. But..."

"Yes?"

She traced a finger along his collarbone and she could feel his body lean into her at the touch. "Cam and Marco will be busy tying things up for the next hour or so. If you can find a private room before then, I'll let you cash in that rain check and you can take care of me any way you wish."

He gave her a quick, rough kiss and tugged on her lower lip with his teeth before he released it and said, "I know of at least four places within walking distance."

She shook her head. "Well, at least you always have an escape route."

He stood up and tugged her to her feet. "Yeah, yeah, tease me later. The clock's ticking and I plan on taking you at least three times before I check in with Marco Alvarez and company. Now, grab your gun and let's go."

She smiled, quickly disassembled her gun, and put it in the case before she followed him down the ladder on the side of the building and down the street.

As they walked hand-in-hand down the street, she couldn't help thinking that just a few months ago, she never would've imagined being free not only to be herself, but to have someone love her true self in return.

It might be silly, but after so many years of loneliness, she yearned—no, needed—to hear the words again. Sabrina squeezed Jorge's hand and said, "I love you."

He looked down at her with a smile, tugged her to the side of the nearest building, and leaned his body against hers. His gaze was a mixture of hunger and tenderness, much like the man Jorge Salazar was slowly becoming.

When he spoke, she could feel his hot breath on her cheek. "I might've been flippant up on the roof, but I meant what I said. Without you, I would be lost, bitter, and maybe even dead. I'm going to prove to you every day that I'm worth your love. I never want to let you go, Sabrina, or I might become lost again. I love you."

She knew it was silly, but she couldn't help but blink back tears at his words. She raised her free hand to his face. "I'd be lost without you too, Jorge. Kiss me to remind me I won't be alone again."

He kissed her tenderly at first, before growing rough and demanding. The feel of Jorge surrounding her, his taste in her mouth, and the knowledge of his love reassured her that she wasn't alone, and if she had any say in it all, she never would be again.

Dear Reader:

Thank you for reading *Shadow of Temptation*! I hope you enjoyed Sabrina and Jorge's story. While the next full-length book will focus on Petra and Will, keep an eye out for the Sabrina and Jorge. They'll be back, along with a lot of the other characters in future books.

Would you like to know when my next book is available? (And receive exclusive goodies and information too?) You can sign up for my newsletter at www.jessiedonovan.com or by liking my Facebook page at http://www.facebook.com/JessieDonovanAuthor.

Also, I need to ask you a favor. Word-of-mouth is crucial for any author to succeed. If you enjoyed this book, please consider leaving a review. Even if it's only a line or two, it would be a huge help!

Thank you for spending time with my characters. I hope you return to the world of the *Feiru* in Will and Petra's book (AMT#3, TBD *2015*). While waiting for the next AMT book, you can check out my serialized dragon-shifter series, *Sacrificed to the Dragon*, or maybe *Reclaiming the Wolf*, the first book in my Cascade Shifters series. Make sure to turn the page for a glimpse into my other works.

With Gratitude,
Jessie Donovan

Check out an excerpt from *Sacrificed to the Dragon*:

CHAPTER ONE

Melanie Hall sat in the reception area of the Manchester Dragon Affairs office, tapping her finger against her arm, and wished they'd hurry the hell up. She'd been sitting here for nearly an hour, and with each minute that ticked by, she started to doubt her eligibility. If she didn't qualify to sacrifice herself to one of the British dragon-shifter clans, her younger brother would die; only the blood of a dragon could cure her brother's antibiotic-resistant CRE infection.

A woman dressed in a gray suit emerged from the far doorway and walked toward her. When she reached Mel, the woman said, "Are you Melanie Hall?" Mel nodded, and the woman turned. "Then follow me."

This is it. In a few minutes, she'd know whether her brother Oliver would get the chance to live or if he would die.

Mel rubbed her hands against her black trousers before she stood up and followed the woman. They went down one dull, poorly lit corridor and then turned left to go down another. The woman in the gray suit finally stopped in front of a door that read "Human Sacrifice Liaison" and turned the doorknob. Rather than enter, the middle-aged woman motioned for Mel to go inside. She obeyed, and as soon as she entered the room, the door slammed shut behind her.

A man not much older than her twenty-five years sat at a desk piled high with folders and papers. The room couldn't be bigger than ten feet by ten feet, but it felt even smaller since every available space on the walls was decorated with different maps of the UK. Some were partitioned into five sections, while others had little pins pushed into them. She had no idea what the pins stood for, but the map divided into five represented the five dragon-shifter clans of the United Kingdom—two in England, one in Scotland, one in Northern Ireland, and one in Wales.

One of which might soon be her home for the next six months.

The man cleared his throat and she moved her attention from the walls to his face. When she met his eyes, he said, "Take a seat."

Mel sat down in the faded plush chair in front of his desk and decided waiting was the best strategy. She had a tendency to say the wrong thing at the wrong time, and while she usually didn't mind, right now it could end up costing her brother his life.

The man picked up a file folder and scanned something inside with his eyes, and then set it down. She wanted to scream for him to tell her the results, but she couldn't do anything to upset him. After all, this man would have the final say over her fate.

The man finally started talking. "Ms. Hall, the genetic testing results say that you are compatible with dragon-shifter DNA and should have no problem conceiving one of their offspring. You also cleared all of the extensive psychological tests. If you're still interested in sacrificing yourself, we can begin the final interview."

Mel blinked. Despite her chances being one in a thousand that she could bear a dragon-shifter child, she qualified. Her younger brother would get the needed dragon's blood and be able to live out a long life free of pain; he now had a future.

Tears pricked her eyes and she closed them to prevent herself from breaking down. *Pull yourself together, Hall.* Crying was the last thing she wanted to do right now. She couldn't give the man any reason to dismiss her as a candidate.

"Ms. Hall?"

Mel opened her eyes and gave a weak smile. "I'm sorry, sir. I'm just relieved that my brother will live."

"Yes, yes, the exchange. But we have a lot to cover before we get to the contract specifics, so if you're quite composed, I'll carry on." Mel sat up straight in her chair and nodded. The man continued. "Right. You are healthy, genetically compatible, fertile, unattached, and not a virgin, which are the five requirements needed to qualify. Sacrificing yourself means that you will go to live with Clan Stonefire for a period of six months, and be assigned a temporary male. You will consent to his sexual attentions, and if you become pregnant, you understand that your stay will be extended until after the child is born. If you have any questions, any at all, now is the time to ask them."

She had heard the basics of this before, but now that she'd passed all of the tests, she had a moment of panic. As much as she wanted to save her brother—and she would save him—being assigned to have sex with an unknown male dragon-shifter was more than a little scary. Especially since many human women died in the process of birthing half dragon-shifter babies.

If the death-by-baby aspect wasn't bad enough, she was putting her life on hold to do this. Mel was one thesis away from earning her PhD in Social Anthropology. If she became pregnant and survived the delivery, she wasn't sure she could just give up the child and walk away. Most of the women sacrifices who lived past the delivery did it, but no matter how different the dragon-shifters were from humans, Mel wouldn't be one of them. Family meant everything to her.

And if she didn't give up her child, she would have to give up her dreams in order to spend the rest of her life with Clan Stonefire.

She took a deep breath and remembered her brother Oliver, pale and thin in his sickbed, and her worry dissipated to a manageable level. Even if she became a mother before she'd planned, she would do it three times over to give Oliver a chance to see past his fifteenth birthday.

Still, she wasn't about to pass up this opportunity to ask some questions. The dragon-shifters were extremely private, rarely sharing anything that happened on their land with the public. "I understand consenting to sexual activity, as my main purpose is to help repopulate the dragon-shifters, but what guarantees are in place to ensure I'm not abused or neglected?"

The man leaned back in his chair and steepled his fingers in front of him. "I understand your concern, but the UK Department of Dragon Affairs conducts routine inspections and interviews. Childbearing-related mortality aside, over the last ten years, only one sacrifice has ever received harsh treatment out of hundreds."

With colossal effort, she managed not to think about her fifty-fifty chance of surviving childbirth. "And what about my friends and family? Can I communicate with them?"

"Communication is forbidden for the first six weeks. After that, it is entirely up to your assigned male as to whether you can communicate or not. From experience, the women who made the greatest effort to conceive were awarded the most privileges."

Right. So if she became a sex goddess, she could talk with her family. How she was going to accomplish that—her previous boyfriends had told her she was "good enough" but never fantastic—she had no idea. But she would cross that bridge when she came to it.

"And lastly, when will my brother receive his treatment and when will I leave for the dragons' compound?"

"Once our legal representative has gone through the contract with you and it's been signed and witnessed, a copy will be sent to Clan Stonefire. They should approve it within a matter of days and deliver the vial of dragon's blood to your brother's physician. Normally, you'd be expected to arrive within a week. However, in the case of dying relatives, you're given two weeks to set your affairs in order and to be assured that your brother is recovering. Our office will notify you of the particulars within the next five days."

The man picked up a pen and signed something inside the manila folder on his desk. He picked up a piece of paper and held it out to her. "Since you've had a rational conversation without breaking down or bursting into tears, I think you're mentally sound enough to be sacrificed. If you have no further questions, you can proceed to the legal department."

Even at this late stage of the application process, she now understood how some candidates might be scared off. Hearing about no communication with the outside world as well as how giving birth to a half-dragon baby might kill you was a lot to take in. But Melanie wasn't doing this for herself; she was doing it for her brother. Oliver had had a shitty last few years fighting off cancer only to beat it and end up with a drug-resistant infection that was slowly killing him.

Her funny, clever brother deserved a chance to live and enjoy life.

She reached out and took the paper. She said, "Thank you. I'm still interested. Please tell me where the legal department is located, and I'll go there straightaway."

He gave her the directions. Mel thanked the man before leaving his office and making the necessary turns. As she approached the last turn, she glanced down at the paper in her hands. Toward the bottom of the sheet, the man had checked "approved" and signed his name. Seeing it in black and white started to make the whole situation feel that much more real.

In less than two weeks, she would go to live with the dragon-shifters and be expected to have sex with one of their males.

She took a deep breath and pushed back the sense of panic. She wasn't forced; she had volunteered. While she didn't know how her assigned dragonman would treat her, there was one thing she had to look forward to—the men were rumored to be fit and muscled. For once in her life, Melanie would get to sleep with a strong, hot man. She only hoped he wouldn't be a complete bastard.

==================

Sacrificed to the Dragon
Available Now

For exclusive content and updates, sign up for my newsletter at:
http://www.jessiedonovan.com

Acknowledgments

I can hardly believe this is my third release this year alone! Of course, while I've spent many hours writing, there are a lot of people who helped make this story possible.

As always, thanks to Jayelle Anderson, my friend and critique partner. This story was the hardest one for me to write so far, and she put up with reading the early, crappier versions of Jorge and Sabrina's story. She's a star!

My editor, Virginia Cantrell, is an all-around awesome person who has a knack for pointing out things that weren't explained well enough. As you can imagine, with the amount of secrets that come out in my stories, she's a huge help! Also, thanks to her boss, Becky Johnson of Hot Tree Editing, for her comments and being so easy to communicate with!

You might have noticed the new "look" of the AMT series, and I owe this beautiful transformation to Clarissa Yeo of Yocla Designs. She's fast, she's friendly, and she has massive amounts of talent. Thanks Clarissa!

And lastly, I thank you, the reader. I couldn't do this without you!

ABOUT THE AUTHOR

Jessie Donovan wrote her first story at age five, and after discovering *The Dragonriders of Pern* series by Anne McCaffrey in junior high, she realized people actually wanted to read stories like those floating around inside her head. From there on out, she was determined to tap into her over-active imagination and write a book someday.

After living abroad for five years and earning degrees in Japanese, Anthropology, and Secondary Education, she buckled down and finally wrote her first full-length book. While that story will never see the light of day, it laid the world-building groundwork of what would become her debut paranormal romance, *Blaze of Secrets*.

Jessie loves to interact with readers, and when not traipsing around some foreign country on a shoestring, can often be found on Facebook and Twitter. Check out her pages below:

http://www.facebook.com/JessieDonovanAuthor
http://www.twitter.com/jessiedauthor

And don't forget to sign-up for her newsletter to receive sneak peeks and inside information. You can sign-up on her website:

http:///www.jessiedonovan.com

19056458R00096

Printed in Poland
by Amazon Fulfillment
Poland Sp. z o.o., Wrocław